CW01334699

Behind the Façade

and

Other Stories

by David Chasumba

First published in Great Britain in 2024 by:

Carnelian Heart Publishing Ltd
Suite A
82 James Carter Road
Mildenhall
Suffolk
IP28 7DE
UK

www.carnelianheartpublishing.co.uk

Copyright ©David Chasumba 2024

Paperback ISBN   978-1-914287-59-6
Hardback ISBN   978-1-914287-60-2

A CIP catalogue record for this book is available from the British Library.

This collection of short stories is entirely a work of fiction. The names, characters and incidents portrayed in it are the work of the author's imagination. Any resemblance to actual persons, living or dead, is purely coincidental.

All rights reserved. No part of this publication may be reproduced, stored in a retrieval system, or transmitted in any form or by any means, electronic, mechanical, photocopying, recording or otherwise without prior written permission from the publisher.

Editors:
Memory Chirere &
Samantha Rumbidzai Vazhure

Cover design & Layout:
Rebeca Covers

Typeset by Carnelian Heart Publishing Ltd
Layout and formatting by DanTs Media

Table of Contents

Out of the Lion's Den	9
Little Rebel Without a Cause	24
The Homecoming	33
Tomb of the Unknown Soldier	55
Dark and Lovely	66
A Sobering Encounter	76
Keep on Trying	79
Behind the Façade – a novella	88
Acknowledgements	198
Biography of David Chasumba	200

For Loveness *Mrs. Loveness*, David (jnr) *Tutu*, Joseph Tendai *Jojo*, Ropafadzo *Roro* and Anesu *Shushu* or *Nesu Nesu*. For my late parents; Sainett Garamukanwa Chasumba and Bessie Dhliwayo Chasumba. For the entire Chasumba family, the Zveushe family, the Mugwara family, Mutyambizi family, Mudzingwa family, Marashe family, Ndirigu family, Chakanyuka family, Mr. and Mrs. Shoko and family, Albert Mativenga and family, James Muramani and family and Stan Mukwenya and family and many people who know me. For Samantha Rumbidzai Vazhure and the Carnelian Heart Publishing family. Thanks for the support.

"Certain kinds of trauma visited on peoples are so deep, so cruel, that unlike money, unlike vengeance, even unlike justice, or rights, or the goodwill of others, only writers can translate such trauma and turn sorrow into meaning, sharpening the moral imagination.

A writer's life and work are not a gift to mankind: they are its necessity."

Toni Morrison, Mouth Full of Blood.

Out of the Lion's Den

It was not Tambudzai who heard the news over the radio first because she was outside the house busy washing piles of dirty laundry by the sink with her smartphone on charger, inside the house.

Instead, it was Mai Kuda, Tambudzai's friend, and neighbour who heard the news first. She came sprinting through the gate like Usain Bolt. 'Did you hear the news, Tambu?' she was gasping for air. She smiled like she had won the lottery.

'What news, *vasikana*?' Tambudzai asked.

'He is being released today!'

'Who?'

'Lawrence. Your husband will be freed from Chikurubi maximum prison today.'

'Ah, *vasikana*, Mai Kuda, please stop kidding me,' Tambudzai stopped washing a dirty skirt and looked at her and then into space.

'I am not kidding you,' Mai Kuda panted.

'Where did you hear this news, before me?' Tambudzai shook her head.

'It was announced, on the noon radio news bulletin, that Supreme Court judges ruled in an urgent appeal court hearing, that Lawrence is not guilty of causing grievous bodily harm to the police officer, and so he must be immediately released from prison.'

'Oh, my God! I don't believe this. Has Jehovah finally answered my prayers?' Tambudzai threw her hands onto her gaping mouth. She held her chest. The sudden surge of blood to her heart unhinged her mind. She dumped the skirt in the sink and dashed into the house.

Inside the lounge, Tambudzai grabbed her smart phone and found five missed calls from Stella, Lawrence's defence lawyer. Her heart thumped.
She phoned Stella. 'Oh no! Her mobile phone is engaged.' She sighed and frowned.

'Try again,' Mai Kuda was staring at the doubting Tambudzai.

Tambudzai phoned Stella's number again. It was still engaged. She didn't want to leave her a voice mail message.

'Try Stella's law firm and speak to one of her partners.'

Tambudzai was relieved when the call went through to Mukurumbira and Partners law firm. Stella's secretary answered the call. She confirmed that Lawrence was indeed due for release that Friday afternoon. And Stella had rushed to Chikurubi Maximum Prison with the release order from the Supreme Court judges, to secure his freedom before the close of business for the weekend. She advised Tambudzai to go immediately to Chikurubi Maximum Prison and wait for Lawrence's release.

'God is good! He finally answered my prayers!' Tambudzai suddenly broke into song and shimmied around the lounge with Mai Kuda, full of excitement. Tears of joy streamed down her cheeks.

After that, Tambudzai changed into a smart navy-blue polka dot dress. She hugged Mai Kuda and rushed to board a commuter omnibus into Harare city central business district. There, she would board a connecting commuter omnibus to

Chikurubi Maximum Prison, situated on the outskirts of the city.

***

Tambudzai had fainted in court the day the High Court Judge pronounced that Lawrence was guilty of causing grievous bodily harm to a police officer and sentenced him to nine years in prison. Two court attendants had stretchered her out of court and provided her with first aid.

How could that be? This was a travesty of justice. Lawrence was innocent. He was nowhere near the crime scene, the shopping centre where opposition party supporters surrounded and bashed one of the police officers who had tried to disperse a rally. He had been home with Tambudzai instead.

The police officer had been left for dead. He had been rushed to Mai Sally Mugabe hospital. He had recovered but was wheelchair bound for life.

Tambudzai had provided her witness statement before the High Court Judge, vouching that Lawrence was at home with her at the time the crime was committed. Three state witnesses had come forward and identified Lawrence. Stella had argued that it was a clear case of mistaken identity and that all these were unreliable state witnesses. But the Judge had sided with the prosecution.

Tambudzai did not understand the judge's nonchalance.

'I think there is judicial capture of the courts by the ruling party,' Stella had hinted. 'The High Court Judge is under orders from powers high up, to silence Lawrence because he is the most vocal leader of the opposition party in the high-density suburb. Nevertheless, I will lodge an immediate appeal against the conviction and sentence with the Supreme Court.'

***

'Mum, where is daddy?' Batsirai, Tambudzai's seven-year-old son, had asked her at dinner on the day of Lawrence's conviction.

'Daddy found a new job in South Africa, and he left immediately.'

'Why did daddy leave without saying goodbye?' Simba, Tambudzai's nine-year-old son, glared at her.

'Daddy had to go. He will be back by Christmas time, when he is off work.'

Batsirai and Simba's faces were sad.

'Boys, I am not feeling well,' Tambudzai had said. 'I am going to bed early tonight.'

Inside the bedroom, Tambudzai had soaked her pillow with a torrent of tears. *Why Lord, why was Lawrence in prison for a crime he did not commit? How would she tell her boys that daddy was in prison and locked up for a crime he didn't commit? How would they react? How would she provide the bread and butter for the boys? Lawrence had always been the breadwinner. Would she manage?*

The first days of Lawrence's incarceration were hard. Tambudzai had missed him a lot. She missed his companionship, the division of labour in the house and his good sense of humour.

Outside the house Tambudzai had to put up with the sympathetic gazes of neighbours and muted whispers of strangers who recognised her on the street. She had ignored them. Mai Kuda had been a loyal friend, always available to listen to her cries and offer emotional support.

She had begun reading the bible daily and attending church regularly with the boys and interceding daily in prayer for Lawrence. It had been sad to sit in church without Lawrence.

But the court appeal had dragged on. Christmas was fast approaching. Tambudzai had started to lose faith in justice for Lawrence. She had wondered what to say to the boys when daddy didn't show up at Christmas time. Nevertheless, she had redoubled her efforts to become the best mum she could be, for Simba and Batsirai. She had sold vegetables and fruits at the local market.

The prison visits had been heart breaking for Tambudzai, especially that she hated seeing the gaunt frame of Lawrence in the prison uniform. But Lawrence had not felt sorry for himself. He had avoided talking politics.

Instead, he had developed a passion for reading the bible in his prison cell and quoting bible verses during the prison visits. Lawrence had encouraged Tambudzai to continue reading the bible and interceding for him in prayer. She had told him that she would do so. He had always given her bible verses to go home and read.

On one occasion he had narrated the bible story of Daniel in the lion's den. Tambudzai had never heard this story narrated that way before. Lawrence had explained how God would save him from the mouth of the hungry lions.

Tambudzai had agreed with him. But in her mind, she had thought Lawrence was going off his rocker. She had not wanted to tell him that he was losing his marbles. She had wanted to be pleasant to him and leave him happy and reassured that he was still loved. She had been happy for him, that he had found an inner strength and peace to cope with his incarceration. Crisis situations always reveal inner strength inside the human being to cope with the distress.

It was ironic that Lawrence, who was languishing in prison, was now the one strengthening Tambudzai spiritually. She was losing hope that her prayers would be answered.

Lawrence had not wanted the boys to know that he was in prison, nor would he have allowed them to visit him because he had not wanted them to see him in a sorry state, wearing the prison uniform. He had written letters to them. He had always reassured them how much he loved and missed them.

Tambudzai had kept him informed about the progress of the boys in school. She had brought him the end of school term reports. They had both been doing well in school. Lawrence would reread their school reports. She had been happy to see him smile. She had known that these minor successes of the boys in school kept him happy and strengthened his spirit and resilient.

She had reassured him that she still loved him until death separated them. He had sobbed every time she had told him that she still loved him. 'I still love you too,' he had muttered, almost choking on his words.

***

'Why is dad not home for Christmas?' Simba asked.

'He will come when he has earned enough money to return home,' Tambudzai put on a bland smile. But a tennis ball blocked her throat.

She went into the bedroom and brought Christmas gifts for Simba and Batsirai. 'Daddy sent these gifts from South Africa.'

Simba fastened his eyes on her. 'Mum, tell me the truth. Is daddy actually in prison?'

'No. Who told you that?'

'My school friends told me that. They heard that from their parents. Mum, please tell me the truth, where is daddy?'

Tambudzai suddenly broke down and sobbed. After she regained composure, she said, 'Yes, daddy is in prison convicted of a crime that he did not commit. Stella, his lawyer, has appealed to the Supreme Court against the conviction and sentence. The appeal has dragged on for far too long. I have visited dad in prison, and he is holding up strong. He loves you two boys with his whole heart. I am sorry that I didn't tell you the truth sooner. It was painful to do so. Besides, I also wanted to protect you from the pain of knowing the truth.'

Simba started to sob.

Tambudzai hugged and caressed him on the head, until he had stopped sobbing. The weight of lying had been lifted off her chest. Simba would tell Batsirai about dad's imprisonment.

***

When Tambudzai got off the commuter omnibus in Harare, she was overwhelmed with joy. She bought a new tracksuit for Lawrence. He had lost weight, but that would fit him well. Then she boarded a commuter omnibus to Chikurubi Maximum Prison from the noisy city centre rank.

Along the way the commuter omnibus burst a rear tyre. 'Is this a bad omen?' Tambudzai wondered.

It took thirty more minutes of arguments before the bus driver agreed to refund the commuter fares to Tambudzai and the other passengers. She waved down another commuter omnibus and boarded it. She was relieved. She didn't want to miss Lawrence's release from prison.

When Tambudzai arrived at Chikurubi Maximum Prison, a large crowd of opposition party supporters had congregated outside the main entrance. The diehard supporters were singing revolutionary songs and dancing. They donned yellow party gowns and waved party flags. Hordes of journalists jostled for vantage points to cover the story.

Trucks full of grim-faced riot policemen in full combat gear, were parked a short distance from the crowd. The atmosphere was pervaded by tension between the vociferous opposition party supporters and the hawk-eyed riot police.

Blood pumped fast to Tambudzai's heart. The atmosphere was surreal to her. She felt overjoyed to see all the opposition party members here to support her family.

Lawrence was leaving prison today and she was taking him home. She couldn't believe it. Tonight, he was sleeping beside her in bed. She had slept alone for three years. She imagined what it would feel like to be caressed by him. She wondered how Batsirai and Simba would react when they saw their daddy back home after his long absence. She was almost peeing herself with excitement.

'Finally, Lawrence, will be free,' said a woman donning a yellow opposition party gown. She shook Tambudzai's hand.

'Thank you for your unwavering support,' Tambudzai smiled and hugged her.

More opposition party supporters arrived at the prison gate. They mobbed Tambudzai and congratulated her on Lawrence's imminent release.

Tambudzai wanted to urge caution, but she realised that this was not the time to dampen the joyous mood with the words of a devil's advocate.

Eventually, Stella, Lawrence's defence lawyer, emerged alone from the prison. She was dressed in a navy-blue outfit and black stilettos. She had a black wig. She addressed the frenzied crowd. 'Thank you all for coming. Good to see you here, Tambudzai. Thank you, opposition party supporters for coming here to support our comrade, Lawrence. Thank you, journalists, for coming to cover this story about a travesty of justice. Lawrence has been in prison for three years for a crime he didn't commit. What are the riot police doing here? We didn't invite them here. We have been slightly delayed by the bureaucratic processes of the prison governor. But we are confident that Lawrence will be released within the next hour. Thank you.'

Stella came to Tambudzai and hugged her. 'We did it! We did it!'

'Thank you, Stella, for your hard work to secure his release.'

'The Supreme Court judges accepted Lawrence's mobile phone activity records from a nearby cell phone tower that located him at home during the time the crime was committed. They dismissed both conviction and sentence.'

They wept in each other's arms and soaked in the reality of Lawrence's impending release.

'Thank you,' Tambudzai smothered tears. She handed Stella the plastic bag with the new tracksuit for Lawrence. 'I hope this tracksuit fits him.'

'I must go back and bring Lawrence out of this godforsaken place.' Stella walked back through the gate into the prison.

Tambudzai paced up and down, with arms akimbo. She constantly glanced at the main prison door. She was heartened that she had a shorter time to wait now. She had waited for this moment for three years.

After an hour that seemed like eternity, Lawrence eventually emerged from the prison door flanked by Stella. He held a plastic bag of his few belongings. He smiled and waved at the wild crowd.

Tambudzai ran into his arms. She kissed and caressed his face. She wept in his arms. There was a roar of jubilation and ululation. The cameras kept flashing.

Lawrence hugged and kissed jubilant opposition party supporters. Tears of joy poured from his eyes like a waterfall.

After he regained his composure, Lawrence addressed the crowd, 'I am very happy to be free and going home to my family. I can't wait to see Simba and Batsirai. It's been three years since I last saw them. There was a travesty of justice. But thank God, justice has been served. I have emerged from the lion's den unscathed like Daniel.' There was a rapturous applause from the crowd.

Tambudzai stood proudly beside Lawrence like a dutiful wife. She loved his oratory skills.

The riot police jumped out of the trucks and began to congregate. Their activity grew more menacing.

'How did you manage to provide for the family during Lawrence's incarceration?' a newspaper journalist asked Tambudzai.

'Times were tough, but I managed. But I don't know how I managed it. It was by the grace of God. I am overjoyed that Lawrence is out of prison. We can go home together and be a complete family again. We must rebuild our family life after this ordeal.'

'Are you going to seek damages from the state for the wrongful imprisonment?' another journalist asked Lawrence.

'The issue of damages will be discussed between me and my legal team. Today, I am only celebrating that I am free at last.'

'How did you keep going in prison?'

'I found my faith inside prison. I read the bible and prayed a lot. That helped me to maintain hope that one day God would hear my prayers and I would be released and be reunited with my family. It wasn't easy keeping my spirits high when I knew I was unjustly imprisoned.'

Tambudzai smothered tears.

It was the crack of dusk. The grim-faced riot police were visibly impatient with the rowdy crowd. They expected the crowd to disperse. But more people kept arriving.

Tambudzai wished the journalists could stop asking Lawrence more unnecessary questions such as what he would do first when he arrived home or what favourite meal he would eat tonight, now that he was a free man.

'I will certainly have a warm bubble bath, and then have quality time with Tambudzai and the boys. I would like to eat a well-cooked meal of *Sadza*, stew and greens. I didn't like the dog food served here in Chikurubi.'

While Lawrence was happy with the media attention, Tambudzai was growing impatient with the media circus. She longed for a quieter, private family space and time. She looked at the riot police. They started advancing on the crowd in a formation.

'Time to disperse now!' A riot police officer announced through a loudspeaker. The police officers began to strike their palms and boots with baton sticks, and they lifted their heavy shields.

'*Voetsek you*! *Voetsek you*!' The crowd cursed the riot police officers.

The riot police officers charged forward.

'Please vacate this area now!' the police officer bellowed again through the loudspeaker.

The crowd stood still. There was a standoff. One of the riot police officers fired a tear gas canister into the crowd. There was a thick plume of smoke and an overpowering odour of tear gas. The diffusing gas stung the eyes and floods of tears poured out.

The crowd scuttled into buses, lorries and cars as the riot police fired more tear gas and beat the people who were not moving. There was a stampede as people fled from the riot police who were whipping them with their baton sticks.

Tambudzai and Lawrence fled with Stella to her car.

As Stella drove through the thick smog of tear gas, Tambudzai held Lawrence's hand tight and squeezed it. She rested her head on his shoulder. She longed for a tranquil family time with Lawrence, Simba and Batsirai, far from the rowdy crowd and rampaging riot police.

She would provide Lawrence with a warm, bubble bath to wash away the prison stench. Then she would cook his favourite dish, sumptuous *sadza*, stew and greens.

Tambudzai longed for the private, intimate moment with Lawrence inside their bedroom. She longed for the pillow talk. She longed for the French kiss of his lips. She longed for the touch of his hard hands caressing the contours of her body. She longed for the warmth of his body on top of her. She longed for the tango of their bodies in a passionate dance of voracious desire and love making. She longed for much more. She smiled in anticipation.

Reunion

I didn't see her first. She spotted me first, and suddenly yelled, 'O my God! David, is that you?'

I turned around. And there she was, standing beside the shelves of breakfast cereals, inside Tesco supermarket. She wore no makeup, and her hair was unkempt like a tramp. She wore a stained white T-shirt with black leggings and dirty trainers.

I didn't recognise her. So, I feigned a smile.

'David, don't you remember me? Jackie Allen. GCSE class of 2000, Bexhill Academy.' She pushed her buggy towards me. There was a baby in the buggy. And another young child clung to her side.

'O, yeah. Now I remember. Jackie. You look so different.'

Jackie Allen, the IT girl. Ringleader of racist class bullies.

She grinned through her tobacco-stained teeth.

'How are you, Jackie?'

'Fine. I am a mother of two now. This is Gemma, five.' Gemma hid behind Jackie. 'And this is baby Nicola, two months old.'

'These are very cute children,' I smiled politely at the kids.

'Do you have any children yourself?'

'No children. Not yet married.' I cleared my throat.

'What do you do for a living now, David?'

'I am an award-winning and best-selling Author.'

Jackie kneeled down to Gemma. 'This is a good friend of mine from school. He writes books and makes lots of money. I am so proud of him.'

No, you weren't a good friend of mine in school, you weasel. Don't you remember calling me a gollywog, all the time? That really hurt. Now the tables have turned.

I took out a twenty-pound note from my wallet and kneeled down to Gemma. I showed her the crisp bank note.

'Say thank you,' Jackie fastened her eyes on Gemma.

'Thank you,' Gemma muttered. She was shy.

'Now listen to me, Gemma,' I said, waving the note and looking her directly in the eyes. 'Promise me, one thing, one thing only. Be a good girl in school. Don't bully other kids in school like your mother did to me and others.' I handed her the pound note.

I stood up and gazed at Jackie.

Her countenance fell and mouth gaped.

'Good day, Jackie,' I said walking away. I remembered a saying from a women's magazine, 'Bullies are like sandpaper - the more they wear you down, the more polished you become.'

Little Rebel Without a Cause

'Tapiwa, please stop it! Pack it in.' Mrs. Henwood barked. She stopped teaching about the vowels on the blackboard and looked daggers at me through her thick lenses.

I stopped fidgeting and sat upright in my small chair. She continued teaching. I punched John in the back.

'He punched me, Mrs. Henwood!' John screamed.

'No, I didn't,' I feigned shock.

'Yes, you did.'

'No, I didn't. Liar, liar. Your pants are on fire,' I made ugly faces at John.

'Tapiwa, stop misbehaving, please. And will you please zip your lips, please?'

'Yes, Mrs. Henwood,' I shifted in my chair and sat still.

'See you outside at breaktime,' John scowled and gestured at me with a clenched fist.

***

I strolled over to John at breaktime. 'Why were you gesturing at me with a clenched fist, you teacher's pet? You want to fight me? Bring it on then.'

John put his lunch box on the bench, 'Piss off, crazy, class clown.'

'Who are you calling a crazy, class clown?' I raised my voice.

'You, loser.'

'You're Mrs. Henwood's poodle,' I countered.

John peeled a banana and ate it. 'Care for a bite? I heard you blacks like bananas.' He muttered some monkey chants.

'Who are you calling a monkey?'

John giggled and strolled away.

I followed him. I tapped him on the shoulder. When he turned around, I slapped him hard across the face and he fell backwards. He got up and punched me hard on the cheek. I fell down and saw twinkling stars.

I got up and slapped John. A fight ensued.

The other children cheered us on as blows and slaps flew.

Mrs. Henwood heard the noise, and she came running to the playground. 'Stop it now, you two!'

John and I were wrestling in the dust. The wrestling match stopped as soon as we heard Mrs. Henwood screaming.

I dusted my uniform.

'Who started the fight?'

'He did,' I pointed at John.

'No, Mrs. Henwood. He hit me first,' John countered. His white face had turned pink with rage.

Mrs. Henwood turned to the other children. 'Tell me the truth, who started the fight?'

All the children on the playground pointed at me. She heard different versions of the same story from the other children, John, and me.

In the end, Mrs. Henwood turned to me, 'I have had it up to my eyeballs with you, Tapiwa. You are such a naughty, little rebel without a cause. What do you have to say for yourself?'

'But he started it, Mrs. Henwood. He called me a class clown and then offered me a banana while making monkey chants. Please believe me, ma'am.'

'I don't believe you.' She grabbed me by the scruff of the neck and forced me back to the classroom.

Back in class, Mrs. Henwood paced around her desk. She gazed into my eyeballs and frowned. 'I've had enough of your disruptive behaviour, Tapiwa. Choose; either to go to the Head Teacher's office to explain why you are always misbehaving in my class or you stand in the naughty corner with a cello tape covering your mouth. Choose now.' She was shaking with anger and breathing into my face. I froze with fear.

I chose to stand in the naughty corner with my mouth muzzled by cello tape. I knew that I would be whipped in the Head Teacher's office.

So, I stood for two hours in the naughty corner, with my big ego deflated like a football, until the end of school.

***

'How was school?' my dad asked me during supper.

'I got into a fist fight with a white kid called John. He called me a monkey. I wasn't taking it and fought him. I tried to explain to Mrs. Henwood that he had provoked me first. But she didn't believe me. Instead, I spent two hours standing in the naughty corner with a cello tape over my mouth.'

'What? I can't believe this. How dare this white teacher put cello tape on your mouth! Why didn't she also reprimand the white kid for the monkey chants? She is probably prejudiced against you. These white teachers all behave the same towards black kids. They can't adapt to teaching in a newly independent, multiracial, Zimbabwe.'

'Calm down, will you. I don't think she is racially prejudiced. She was just trying to discipline Tapiwa,' my mother interjected. 'You know very well that he can be quite a handful.'

'I won't allow this white teacher to humiliate my child like that, in independent Zimbabwe. I will see her tomorrow morning and demand an explanation from her. I spent time in political detention. I was humiliated by sadistic detention guards. I won't allow this prejudiced white teacher to humiliate my son, that way. This is no longer Rhodesia. We are now living in a free Zimbabwe.'

'You must go to the school and find out the whole truth from the teacher,' my mother said. 'Please don't yell at her, please don't.'

My dad stood up. He was breathing heavily. He stormed off to the kitchen.

At bedtime, my mother came to my bedroom. She knelt beside my bed. 'Please don't listen to your dad. He is a bitter man. He was detained by the Ian Smith regime for involvement in Black Nationalist politics. We now live in an independent Zimbabwe, built on reconciliation and tolerance of the different races. You must go and say sorry to John and be friends with him. It pleases God when you forgive your enemies.'

'Yes, mother.'

That night I couldn't sleep. I felt guilty that I had not told the whole truth and got Mrs. Henwood in trouble with my crazy dad. Now my class mischief would be known by my parents.

***

It was a privilege to attend multiracial, Frank Johnson Primary School in 1980. The school, located in a low-density residential suburb, had previously been for white children only during the white colonial Ian Smith regime.

It had been named after Frank Johnson, the leader of the Pioneer Column, a colonial army that colonised the country and named it Rhodesia.

After independence, my black family had moved into the white low-density suburb where the school was located. It was a shock for me to move from the noisy, overcrowded black townships to the quiet, white low-density suburb with manicured lawns, big houses, and yards.

The only white person I knew then was our elderly neighbour who resented black families moving into the former white's only neighbourhood. She had called the police on many occasions because we, black kids, made noise and marked out the tarmac when we played childhood games. I hated the racially prejudiced, old white woman.

My father had insisted that I should attend Frank Johnson Primary because it was multiracial. But I wasn't prepared for the shock of learning in such a school. It was a whole new learning experience.

On the first day of school, I wore smart mint uniform, white socks, and polished Bata shoes, with a green jersey, and green and yellow tie. 'You are looking really smart,' my dad had said as he drove me to school.

I immediately loved the stunning panoramic view of the school; the spacious and well-ventilated white classrooms, lush lawns, clean swimming pool and sports fields on many acres of land.

On the first day, I was quiet in class because I couldn't speak proper English nor clearly understand it. The white kids thought I was dumb and immediately picked on me. I had felt stupid, sad, and scared of their blue eyes.

I was so unhappy that I had cried all through break time and asked the teacher to call my dad. He had taken me home.

'You will fit in better when you can speak better English,' my dad had reassured me.

The following week had been better. I had started improving my English-speaking and listening skills. I had made new friends and adjusted to the routines of the school. I was much happier.

One day my dad was offended when I told him that Mrs. Henwood had taught us how to eat and speak properly. 'Why should she teach you how to eat properly? You are not an empty vessel that needs lessons on how to eat quietly? She should respect the culture you bring from home.' My dad was not amused.

'I don't think she meant any harm. She is a good teacher,' my mother had chipped in. 'She wants him to learn to eat quietly, not like a cow chewing the cud. There is a lot Tapiwa can learn from her.' My dad shook his head in disbelief.

In class, I craved for Mrs. Henwood's attention. But she didn't always give it to me. She saw me as a little rebel with a poor attitude who needed to improve behaviour and concentration in class.

So, she always reprimanded me, 'Tapiwa, will you please zip your lips, please? Will you please sit still and pay attention, please? Seek permission to leave the class. Tuck in your shirt and socks. Eat properly, chew quietly, swallow bread and then drink the milk. Stop speaking in Shona in class.'

I hated her picking on me all the time. It was unfair.

On the contrary, Mrs. Henwood loved praising her class poodle. 'You must all behave like John. He is intelligent, and well dressed. He has good manners.'

My head ached every time she quaked on and on about John this, or John that.

Obviously, it upset me that I had failed to live up to her expectations. So, I decided to rebel against her class rules and fulfil her expectations of me.

On rare occasions I got the attention that I craved from her. I cherished those moments because they made me happy and improved my self-esteem.

Soon, two groups developed inside and outside the classroom. One group, comprising mostly the white kids, was well behaved in class and well-liked by Mrs. Henwood. This group, which included my sworn class enemy, John, was more active in class.

Naturally, I belonged to the second group of rebels, mostly black kids not liked by Mrs. Henwood. On the playground, my group was bossier and louder. I yelled, 'Teacher's poodle,' every time I bumped into John at break time in the playground. I loved to see his face turn pink with anger.

***

The following morning my dad drove me to school. He left me at the threshold of the class door. An hour later, I was called to the Head Teacher's office. My dad was sitting in the office.

The Head Teacher asked me who had caused the fight in the playground. I was tongue tied. I was relieved when my dad spoke on my behalf.

'But you must not fight in the playground. Do you hear me?' The Head Teacher glared at me. I nodded.

Mrs. Henwood was called to the office, and she explained that I was disruptive in class, and that she had tried different ways of disciplining me, but I was difficult to manage during lessons.

My dad said it was not right though to put cello tape on a child's mouth and make him stand in the naughty corner for two hours.

Mrs. Henwood apologised for her actions, and she said that wouldn't happen again. I returned with her to the classroom.

Outside the classroom door, Mrs. Henwood stopped. She looked me in the eyes and put her hand on my head. She caressed my head. 'I am deeply sorry about putting cello tape on your mouth and banishing you to the naughty corner.'

I didn't say anything. Tears sparkled in my eyes.

'You and I must have a fresh start,' she continued. 'You must behave yourself inside my classroom and I will support you. If you don't improve your naughty behaviour, and continue being a little rebel without a cause, I will phone your dad and tell him about everything. I want you to become a good boy.'

'Yes, ma'am.' I nodded. We entered the classroom.

That evening, at home, I learnt that my crazy dad had threatened to sue Mrs. Henwood for putting cello tape on my mouth. He called it racist abuse. So, the Head Teacher and Mrs. Henwood had been forced to apologise. My dad had bragged about having the best white lawyer in the city of Harare.

I understood why my dad reacted the way he did. He was entitled to his own views. I also understood why Mrs. Henwood behaved the way she did. She had the right to maintain good behaviour in her class. But sealing my mouth with cello tape horrified my dad.

I was left with no option but to behave myself in class. I didn't want Mrs. Henwood phoning my crazy dad about my mischief in class.

From that day onwards, Mrs. Henwood behaved differently towards me. She was kinder and more considerate when she spoke to me. She was quick to compliment me when I did well during the lessons.

I began to trust and respect her more. I did everything to please her. At the end of the school term, I was awarded a book prize for the most improved child in her class.

The Homecoming

'Please do something, Samira,' Andrew pleaded over the phone. 'I can't be deported.' He shivered in the cold morning breeze.

'Yes, I will lodge a final appeal this morning. I also don't want you to be deported to Zimbabwe tonight. But the complication is your asylum law violation. Your application was rejected twice because of that violation. But the final decision on whether to deport you lies in the hands of the judge today. I hope he will grant you a last-minute right to stay in the UK.'

'You are my last hope, Samira. I am desperate. Please, argue that I'm at risk of incarceration if I returned to Zimbabwe.'

'I will do that, Andrew. Pray that you are not on that chartered flight leaving Gatwick for Harare tonight at 10:30pm. I will phone you at 2pm with the judge's verdict.'

The impending deportation of Zimbabwean illegal migrants was headline news in all the UK media. Some people felt that it was the right move for the UK government to deport 'illegal immigrants.' Some migration and human rights organisations, charities and politicians in the UK were more sympathetic towards the migrants and challenged the deportation in the High Court. They argued that the deportees were at risk of persecution if they were returned to Zimbabwe.

However, the Home Secretary defended the impending deportations. "The United Kingdom has a right to deport illegal Zimbabweans migrants who committed serious crimes such as murder, rape and other petty crimes."

The Home Affairs Minister from Zimbabwe had rubbed salt into the wounds of the illegal migrants. He came to England and dismissed as "unfounded," the fears that the deportees faced persecution back home. "We will warmly welcome home all our Zimbabwean citizens," he had said.

Andrew prayed for divine intervention, pleading with God to spare him from deportation. He read the bible scriptures about God rescuing the Israelites from the hand of evil Pharoah. He hummed the hymn, *Abide with me*.

He sat up on the small bed in his room at the detention centre and watched the news. There was more intense fighting in the Donbas region in Ukraine. He switched off the tv. He shuffled around in his room like a cornered mouse. He hoped that a last-minute reprieve would save him from deportation. He didn't want to leave his girlfriend, Holly and their one-year-old daughter, Chloe. He glanced at his phone constantly. Time was slow. There was an emptiness inside his belly. His intestines twisted. He scrolled through his phone messages and put the phone down. He fell asleep.

Then the phone rang in the afternoon. Andrew's heart thumped hard on the walls of his rib cage. It was Samira.

'I am sincerely sorry, Andrew, Justice Steyn declined your final appeal. He has made an order that you must be removed from England tonight. He opined that your fears of persecution in Zimbabwe were unfounded. Therefore, you must be deported.'

'Oh, no!' Andrew put his hand on his head.

'I'm sincerely sorry. I tried my best. But it was in vain. Good luck with the future, Andrew.'

'Gosh! Thank you, anyway, for your help, Samira. Thank you.'

Samira ended the call.

'Damn!' Andrew threw the phone on the bed and punched the air in anger. He was deranged. Tears filled his eyes. His worst fears had been confirmed. He was being deported back to Zimbabwe tonight after five years of striving for a better life in England. But his dreams were now up in smoke. Dreams deferred. He fell onto the bed and sobbed. He cupped his face in his hands. He wiped streams of tears flowing down the contours of his cheeks. Then he fell asleep.

There was a hard knock on the door. 'Come in.'

A Border Enforcement Officer walked in and handed Andrew some forms.

'What is this?'

'Deportation forms. Please sign here.'

'No. I am not doing that.'

'Justice Steyn has ordered your deportation. You must sign these forms.'

'I don't agree with the deportation. So, why should I sign these forms?'

'Well, you don't have a choice, but to sign them. You will be on board that chartered flight back to Zimbabwe tonight anyway. The van leaves for Gatwick in an hour.'

'White bastard!'

'What did you say?'

'I said kiss my ass.'

The officer frowned. 'You don't have to vent your anger on me. I didn't make the order to deport you. Justice Steyn did. I am just doing my job. Now can you please sign these forms, please?'

'Yeah, right, you're doing your bloody job. Doing your fucking job. You are deporting me to a country that I don't want to return to. Yeah, right, doing my job, my fucking foot.'

He snatched the forms from the officer's hands and scribbled his signature. 'There you are. Happy bunny, now?' He threw the forms at the officer.

The officer picked up the forms and stormed out of the room.

Andrew lay on the bed looking up, with hands cupping his head. He sighed and remembered the fish shop raid.

***

It was a bright sunny day. He had gone to work in the kitchen at the chip shop as usual. Suddenly, immigration officers stormed into the chip shop during the busy lunch hour and sealed off all exits. They ordered the customers out of the shop. They ordered the owner, three other workers, and Andrew into a back room.

'Show us your valid UK visa and work permit.'

The chip shop owner and the three workers had immediately handed over their passports. Andrew fumbled through his pockets and handed him the work permit.

The eagle-eyed immigration officer studied Andrew's permit. 'This is a fake work permit and visa. You are under arrest for living and working illegally in the UK.'

Andrew was handcuffed and forced out of the chip shop to a border control and enforcement van outside. He was humiliated in front of onlookers.

He was charged with violating UK immigration laws. Andrew had countered by applying for asylum for a second time. Now his third and final appeal against deportation had just been rejected. He had prayed for divine intervention, and this had failed. He prayed for the last-minute halting of deportations due to a pending high court appeal by human rights activists and asylum charities.

***

On the small bed, Andrew thought about the strained relationship with his mother. *Would she welcome him home with open arms after what had happened?* His thoughts were interrupted by two bulging, grim faced border enforcement officers who entered the room without knocking. 'Please pack your belongings. We are leaving for Gatwick airport shortly.'

Tears glimmered in Andrew's eyes and flowed down his cheeks. He packed his few belongings; two shirts, a pair of trousers, a green jacket, red cardigan, phone charger, headphones, and big bible into a duffle bag.

'Will you please allow me to see my girlfriend, Holly, and my year-old daughter, Chloe, before I leave?'

'We won't allow that. You will get very emotional and make it difficult for us to enforce the deportation order.'

The officers glared at him, then at each other and giggled.

'What's there to giggle about?' Andrew seethed like a bulldog. He scowled his face. After that, the officers cuffed and escorted him out of Brook House Detention Centre. He stole a final glance at the detention centre and his heart sank.

'I am not going into the van.' Andrew pushed back against the officers.

'Please don't make things harder for yourself,' said one officer.

The two officers forced Andrew into the van and bolted the heavy metal doors of the caged van.

'Racist bastards,' he yelled and spat at them.

The seething officers sat next to him and wiped the spit off their clean shirts. They glared at him like angry lions ready to devour him.

'Pack it in. We will taser you if you make another aggressive act towards us,' said one of the stern officers

Inside the van there were three other handcuffed deportees; a young man, a middle-aged woman and man. The downcast young man was listening to music with his headphones on. He didn't acknowledge Andrew sitting opposite him.

The middle-aged woman sobbed and dabbed her eyes with tissues. 'Why are you treating us worse than dogs?' she asked. She looked at the officers and continued sobbing.

The middle-aged man glared at Andrew and smiled like a madman.

Andrew looked away. *Gosh, what is there to smile about, he wondered. He must have lost the complete function of his mental faculties, he thought.*

Andrew contemplated unshackling his handcuffs and daring a Hollywood movie style escape from the van. But how would he escape from the officers with bulging muscles or the bolted, caged van?

He imagined Holly and Chloe waiting for him in the airport and being denied the last opportunity to bid farewell to him, by border control officers. He called Holly's mobile phone. She didn't answer. He was distraught and left a voicemail message.

It was now dark outside, on the wet winter night.

The van sped along the busy motorway.

Later the van stopped at an entrance to Gatwick airport. The gate was opened after the driver showed the security officer some papers. The van manoeuvred through the bright lights of the road running parallel to the airfield. The van stopped in front of a medium-sized jet.

Two border enforcement officers, from the driver's side, opened the doors of the van and let the other three deportees out first, onto the tarmac. Andrew was left inside the back of the van with the two officers watching him. The deportees were forced up the steps and disappeared into the jet.

'Now your turn,' said one of the officers. The two officers grabbed Andrew under the arms and yanked him out of the van. The bright lights outside blinded Andrew.

'That is not the right way to treat me,' Andrew spat on the ground.

'Will you please shut your mouth!' barked one of the officers. He was led up the steps onto the chartered jet.

Andrew imagined a scene from the film *Con Air* where all the baddies were loaded onto a plane. He would have loved to play the character, Cameron Poe (Nicholas Cage). He was forced to a seat, next to the middle-aged, mad man from the van.

'Don't you have hearts you white folks. Why are you treating us like dogs?' The mad man scowled at the officers.

'I am warning you to please shut up or else.'

'Or else what?'

'Or else I will seal your mouth.'

'Come kiss my doodah.'

Two officers sealed the mad man's mouth with cello tape. Andrew overheard the border guards mutter that the man had become mad after he stabbed his wife and mutilated her body.

Andrew was scared of the mad man. His belly tightened.

The pilot announced that the jet would be delayed due to unforeseen circumstances.

Suddenly the latch on the jet's door was opened. Border enforcement officers entered the plane and walked over to the middle-aged woman who had been sobbing.

'Today is your luckiest day, madam. Justice Steyn has granted a last-minute reprieve and ordered that your deportation be stopped.'

'Thank you, Lord. Thank you, *Mwari*. I couldn't leave my family here in England. Thank you, Lord. *Ndatenda Mwari*.' The woman raised her hands to the heavens and chorused a thank you hymn.

Andrew wished it was him being taken off the jet. But the air hostess latched the door and secured it.

Andrew's phone rang. His heart jumped. It was Holly. 'I have been trying to get hold of you. Why didn't you answer my calls?'

'I am at the airport. Where are you?'

'Inside the jet. The officers said I couldn't see you because I would get very emotional and make their job harder to enforce the deportation order. I will always love you, Holly. Tell Chloe that daddy loves her. I will phone you when I am in Zimbabwe.'

'I love you too, Andrew. I will visit you in Zimbabwe.' Tears flooded Andrew's eyes. 'I love you so much, babe.' He choked on his words.

'Switch off your phone. We are about to take off,' one of the air hostesses said, with a frown on her face.

'Bye, Holly, love you, honey.' Andrew ended the call and wiped away the tears. A snooker ball was lodged on his throat.

Then the jet moved forward and started taxiing towards the runway. Andrew felt a sinking feeling in the pitch of his belly as the jet took off. Floods of tears flowed out of his eyes.

***

Andrew remembered when he came to England with high hopes and expectations and lived on a visitor's visa for the first six months. Thereafter, he lived under the radar without papers, working illegally. He had applied three times for asylum, but his applications were denied.

He wondered whether someone back home had put a bad luck spell on him. *Was it mother or Rumbidzai? Was it God punishing him for dumping pregnant Rumbidzai? Was this a good case of what goes around comes around? Was this his comeuppance?* This was one hell of a homecoming, *helluva homecoming*, with nothing to show for all the time he had lived and worked in England.

When his first immigration lawyer saw his desperation to work, he had introduced Andrew to a dodgy West African man who provided him fake immigration papers. That is how he had ended up working at the chip shop. He was just in the wrong place at the wrong time.

He thought about his mother back in the Harare high density suburb of Mufakose. He had promised to look after her when he left for England, but he had struggled to do so. *Did she curse him to wander the streets like a mad man, kutanda botso?*

He thought about Rumbidzai, his ex-girlfriend. He dumped her and denied paternity of her child. He preferred chasing his diaspora dreams instead. She had given birth to a girl who was now five years old. *Had Rumbidzai remarried? Would she forgive him for dumping her and her child? Would she accept a DNA test to lay to bed the paternity question for good?*

Then he fell asleep. In a dream Rumbidzai and her daughter refused his apology and a DNA test. They chased him away. He woke up with a start. He was relieved that it was only a dream. He rubbed his sleepy eyes. It was quiet inside the cold cabin. There was an engine drone. The lights inside the cabin were dimmed. The mad man and the other deportees were fast asleep.

Andrew peered outside the window, into the misty clouds. He dreaded the jet might crash into what appeared to be an ocean below. And there would never be a trace of his existence on the face of the earth.

He went back to sleep. He saw his mother smiling and welcoming him back home in a dream. She told him that she missed him, and that the ancestors were also happy that he was returning home where his umbilical cord was cut and buried. He was crying in his sleep and asking for forgiveness.

He was woken up. An air hostess asked him if he wanted rice with chicken stew or rice with beef stew. He preferred chicken stew. He asked for a cold can of beer.

He struggled to chew. But he forced himself to eat because he was as hungry as a swine. He took huge sips of the beer and fell asleep.

The pilot announced that the passengers must fasten their seat belts ready for landing at Robert Gabriel Mugabe International airport. His intestines tightened. He wished he had returned home in better circumstances, with family waiting for him in the arrivals hall, cheering and hugging him. But this was not a normal homecoming.

The jet touched down at the airport in the late afternoon. The sky was cloudless, and the sun was high up and baking hot in August. The jet slowly taxied down the runway and stopped, in front of the expanded airport terminal with blue, glinting glass.

Andrew peered outside and saw a swarm of journalists at the airport with cameras lined up. The pilot announced that the jet had arrived, and the passengers must be escorted out by the UK border enforcement officers.

Journalists charged forward as Andrew, the other deportees and UK border control officers descended the steps.

'Why were you deported?' one journalist asked. Andrew quietly walked past him. The mad man spoke to a tv journalist. He was unrepentant about the heinous crime he had committed in England.

The deportees were handed over to the Zimbabwean immigration officers. Andrew stood in the immigration queue.

'We are going to take you to a quarantine centre for 10 days, due to Covid. After that you can go home to your families,' said one female Zimbabwean immigration officer.

Andrew was gutted. He didn't want to stay any longer in detention. He wanted to go home.

The deportees were quickly led to a bus that was headed to an undisclosed quarantine centre. Andrew coughed from the black fumes coming out a worn exhaust pipe of the bus. He wanted his nightmare to end. He could no longer stomach living in yet another detention.

Many questions whizzed through Andrew's head as the bus manoeuvred the roundabout out of the airport. *What would he say to mum when he met her? Would she accept him back home? Would he end up homeless on Harare streets? What would he say to Rumbidzai and her child? What would be the nature of his relationship with Holly and Chloe back in London?*

As the bus passed under the tall, concrete arch crossing the road, Andrew was struck by the bold message written on the arch; **Zimbabwe Independence 1980**. The message had connotations of a new hope, a new beginning. *Was this a clue for him, about a new beginning? Was this a clue for him to swallow his pride, and ask for forgiveness from mum, Rumbidzai and her child? But would they accept his apologies? Would Rumbidzai accept a DNA test to determine the child's paternity?*

He had seen many poignant episodes of the DNA Show, in which the presenter, Tinashe Mugabe, met estranged couples and revealed DNA test results of the child's paternity.

Although Andrew now faced an uncertain future in a country that he no longer had a deep connection with, he was determined to put things right with mum, Rumbidzai and her child. He consoled himself that it was better to return to his ancestral home than continue living in detention in London.

He would soon be free like a bird. He wished the DNA test showed that he had fathered Rumbidzai's child. He would try to create some relationship with the child. It was never too late to mend broken relationships and adapt to a new life back home.

He remembered Holly and Chloe and felt sad. Only time would tell how he would adjust to this new reality, this new life, in Zimbabwe, the house of stone.

We Must Talk

Kudzai manoeuvred his Volvo S40 off the main highway onto a narrow country road. He lowered the window and inhaled fresh, clean English countryside air.

Many questions troubled his mind. *Why did he agree to meet Mr. Arnold, Chloe's dad? Why was he doing so, behind Chloe's back? Was he betraying her trust by meeting her dad in secret? How would she react when she got wind of the secret meeting? How did Mr. Arnold get hold of his mobile number? Was it safe meeting this strange sixty-five-year-old conservative, white man in the middle of nowhere, at a countryside pub?*

'Meet me at 2pm sharp, at the Sportsman Bar on Saturday,' Mr. Arnold had said in a commanding voice. 'You and I must talk, man to man, about your relationship with my Chloe. Don't tell Chloe about this meeting.'

'Why not?'

'It has nothing to do with her.'

'What do you mean, it has nothing to do with her?'

'The meeting is about me laying my cards on the table and expressing how I feel about your relationship with my daughter.'

'Fair enough. Chloe is your daughter. But I happen to be madly in love with her. I will see you then.'

Kudzai remembered Chloe describing her dad as, 'a conservative English farmer who doesn't particularly like the company of people of colour. He is a Tory. He loves hunting and drinking Guinness at the local Sportsman pub on Sunday afternoons with other people who look like him.'

Kudzai voted Labour and hated the *Tory boys*. He thought this would be a good opportunity to meet his future father-in-law and charm him, when Chloe wasn't present.

He wondered how much more Mr. Arnold knew about him; besides that, he was a Black man who emigrated from Zimbabwe and was dating his daughter.

He accelerated along a clear stretch of the country road. It was a sunny, hot, and cloudless day in August. He glanced at large, beautiful farmhouses dotted along the road. He slowed down. There was a slow-moving tractor ahead. He gritted his teeth, impatient with the tractor driver. He was relieved when the tractor turned to the left side road. He accelerated.

He saw the bold Sportsman Pub sign on the right side of the road. He slowed down and turned into the car park. He suddenly became more nervous. *What if Mr. Arnold pulled a gun at him?* He reassured himself that the rendezvous was a safe public place. Besides, it was too late now to turn back and drive back to London. He exhaled. His heart pumped fast.

Kudzai sauntered into the quiet pub with wooden panelling inside. His heart was bursting his rib cage. He glanced at the bartender and then around the pub. He spotted an elderly white man sitting on a table of two, at the far end. There were no other pub patrons. A sensation of fear tugged his senses as he strolled towards the white man.

The man glanced at Kudzai from skull to sole and scowled his face. He wore green corduroy trousers, a green tweed jacket on top of a button up sweater, flat cap, and riding shoes.

'Mr. Arnold? Kudzai.' Kudzai stood close to the man and extended his hand. But the white man didn't extend his hand.

'Yes, Mr. Arnold. Please sit down,' he glared at Kudzai again and beckoned him to the chair.

Kudzai drew out a chair and sat down. He faced Mr. Arnold. 'Who gave you my number?'

'Chloe's mother. Mothers always know what's going on with their daughters.'

There was momentary silence.

'Where have you come from?'

'Brixton, London.'

'Were you always there?'

'No. I moved to Brixton when I was five.'

'Where from?'

'Zimbabwe.'

'Zimbabwe. Mugabe, farm invasions, poverty, corruption, and HIV/AIDS.'

'Zimbabwe is a beautiful country with beautiful people and natural beauty. It is more beautiful than the negative western media stereotypes.'

'So, if your country is so beautiful, why are you living here, and dating my Chloe?'

'I don't think it concerns you why I am living in England. Your concern is why I am dating Chloe. Yes, we are in a serious relationship.'

'How long have you been in this "serious relationship" with her?'

'One year.'

'Where did you meet her?'

'At Sussex Uni.'

'I see.' Mr. Arnold paused and beckoned to a waiter. 'Can I have a Guinness please? Would you like a Guinness?'

'No thanks. I am driving. A glass of water will do. Thanks.' Andrew cleared his throat.

'So, what are your future plans with Chloe?' he gazed at Kudzai.

Kudzai was surprised. 'Chloe and I are just dating. But we haven't made future plans yet.'

'I thought you said you were "in a serious relationship" with my Chloe?'

'Yes, we are. When there are future plans, you will be the first to know.'

'How well do you know Chloe?'

'What do you mean?'

'I mean, have you slept with her?'

'No. Besides, I don't think it is any of your business, whether I slept with her or not.' His face was contorted with disgust.

'Young man, it is my business, when you sleep with my daughter. Now, tell me the truth.' Mr. Arnold raised his voice and beamed his laser eyes into Kudzai's eye sockets.

'Sir, I haven't slept with Chloe. That is the truth.' Kudzai was frightened.

'I don't want my Chloe sleeping around with a black man and bearing brown babies.'

'Well, that should be her choice, not yours. Chloe is twenty-one. I don't see a problem with us, consenting adults, in a relationship.'

'I do have a problem with that. Does your mother approve of your relationship with Chloe?'

'Yes, she does.'

'Well, I strongly disapprove of miscegenation. It was outlawed in the past.'

'Well, thank God, nowadays everyone is free to date and marry whoever they love.'

'But the fact remains, I disapprove of you marrying my Chloe. You should go back to your black land and marry your own kind. Besides, I don't think you can afford to look after my Chloe.'

'Well, Chloe is smart and old enough to decide who she wants to date or marry.'

'She won't have my blessings to marry a black man. That is for sure.'

Kudzai shook his head. 'If we decide to marry, we will do so without your blessings then. Chloe and I love each other, and that is what really matters.'

'Excuse me.' Mr. Arnold stood up and went to the toilet.

Kudzai wanted to walk away at that moment. But he decided to stay. Walking away would be disrespectful. He would take the moral high ground. He remembered Michelle Obama's words, 'When they go low, you go high.' He was determined to win this duel with Mr. Arnold.

Mr. Arnold returned from the toilet and beckoned to the waiter for another Guinness. His face had turned pink. He drew his chair and sat.

'Can you please write your name in full,' he handed Kudzai a pen and piece of paper.

Surprised, Kudzai wrote down his name on the paper.

Mr. Arnold looked at the piece of paper. 'Kudzai Gumbo.' He said that with a posh accent. His face was punctuated by a cynical smile. He whipped out a cheque book and wrote in it.

Kudzai looked on in bewilderment.

He tore the cheque out of the cheque book. 'Here you are. This is for you.'

'What for?' Kudzai took the cheque and looked at it. '£2000! Why are you giving this to me?'

'Well, to compensate you, for the inconvenience of breaking up with my Chloe.'

'This is unbelievable! Holly Mary, mother of Christ! Jesus Christ! You are bribing me to break up with her? That is why you didn't want Chloe to know about this meeting. Gosh! Well, I am not going to break up with her. You may as well shove this cheque down where the sun doesn't shine.' He threw the cheque back at Mr. Arnold. It landed on the floor.

'Win-win situation. Buy Christmas presents for your poor mum and leave my Chloe alone.'

'Chloe is an adult. She makes her own dating decisions. It is ludicrous for you to interfere in her dating. I won't accept the cheque.' Kudzai was frothing in the mouth and shaking his head.

Mr. Arnold picked the cheque off the floor and put it in front of Kudzai. He was smirking.

'I have had enough of this nonsense!' Kudzai was panting like a greyhound.

'You are taking it the wrong way, young man.'

'I must go now.' Kudzai stood up and stormed out of the pub. He cursed under his breath. *Bloody bastard has the cheek to bribe me to break up with his daughter. Jesus Christ!*

Mr. Arnold followed him out of the pub. He was still holding the cheque in his hand.

Kudzai sat in his car and held tight to the steering wheel. He was shaking and hissing like a black mamba.

'You can still take the cheque, you know.' Mr. Arnold stood outside his car in the car park, gazing at him.

Kudzai was lost in thought.

'Sorry if I offended you, by offering you the cheque. I was only looking up for the interests of my daughter like any father should. I really don't want you to ever be my son-in-law.'

Kudzai glanced at Mr. Arnold. 'Alright, Mr. Arnold, I hear you. You don't want me to be your future son-in-law. That is fine. I don't want to have a racist future father-in-law like you either. I don't have an option now, do I? I will take your cheque.' Kudzai feigned a smile. He extended his hand and took the cheque. He put it in his breast pocket. 'Thank you, Mr. Arnold. It was really good talking to you. Please have a pleasant day.'

Kudzai pulled up the window and drove away. It pained him that he had finally met Mr. Arnold, a hard nut to crack. He had accepted the cheque but was determined to win the duel with Mr. Arnold. He felt guilty of betraying Chloe by meeting her father in secret.

Then a thought crossed his mind. Wait a minute. He could still have the last laugh. He could cash the cheque and still remain in a relationship with Chloe. She didn't know about this meeting. He could buy her expensive perfume as a Christmas present. He could book a holiday, an African safari to the Victoria Falls with her. He imagined Chloe and him sitting on benches, sipping Pina Colada, and kissing and seeing the orange sun setting over the Zambezi valley or sitting inside a 4x4 safari truck and watching the wild animals in their natural habitat. There was a lot he could do with the cheque from Mr. Arnold. Or he could just deposit it in his account and earn interest.

***

'What is the matter, Kudzai? You sounded frantic over the phone.' Chloe sat upright in her chair at the table for two in Wetherspoons. 'Have you decided to end our relationship?'

'Hell, no, babe.'

'What's the matter then?'

Kudzai smiled and sipped orange squash. He gazed around the restaurant and cleared his throat. He leaned forward and said, 'We must talk.'

'Talk about what?'

He fumbled with the button of his breast pocket. He hesitated and whipped out the cheque. Then he laid it in front of Chloe.

She picked up the cheque and studied it. 'Cheque? Why did my dad write the cheque to you?'

'That is why I called you to talk.'

'Talk about what?'

'About the cheque.'

'What is going on Kudzai? Why would my dad write you a cheque?'

Kudzai cleared his throat and sipped the squash. He shifted in his chair and kneaded his fingers. His heart was pounding. There was a momentary silence. 'Babe, I went to see your dad.'

'What!' Chloe's face was deformed with shock. 'You what?' She glared at him.

For a moment words were stuck under his tongue. 'Let me explain.' Kudzai exhaled and cleared his throat.

Tomb of the Unknown Soldier

Tererai was kneeling and weeding the grass between the black, shiny granite gravestones at the Heroes Acre cemetery in Harare. Balls of sweat dripped down his face on the sun-baked August afternoon.

It was a week before the Heroes Day celebrations and two weeks before the Presidential elections.

He turned around and saw a man holding a wreath and standing in front of the Tomb of the Unknown Soldier. The man gazed up at the statue and placed the wreath at the foot of the statue. He stepped back and saluted.

Tererai stood up and approached the man. He cleared his throat.

The man jolted back to reality and turned around to face Tererai.

'Good morning, sir.' Tererai smiled at the tall, smartly dressed, middle-aged man with a smooth and lighter skin.

The man smiled. 'I'm Moses. And you?' His smile was friendly.

'Tererai. I am a gardener and general hand here at the Heroes Acre. Pleased to meet you, sir.' He shook Moses's hand.

'Pleased to meet you too, Tererai.'

'Do you live here, in Harare?'

'Yes and no. I have a home here in Harare, but I live in a small quiet English town, Bexhill-on-sea.'

'I could tell from your fluent English accent that you come from the diaspora.'

'Yeah.'

'We don't normally see people from the diaspora come here to lay a wreath at the Tomb of the Unknown Soldier. I hope you don't mind me asking, but what brings you to this Tomb?'

Figure 1: Tomb of the Unknown Soldier in the Heroes Acre, by Yagil Henkin

'My Sekuru Lovemore, the eldest son of my mother's brother, a ZANLA combatant died during the war of liberation, fighting for the freedom of the black people of this country.'

'When did he join the war?'

'1976.'

'Where did your Sekuru come from?'

'A village near Katiyo in Uzumba Maramba Pfungwe.'

'I heard that there were many fierce battles between the ZANLA forces and the Rhodesia army over there.'

'Yes. The ZANLA forces operated in my Sekuru's village with the support of the *Povo* - people of various opinions. But the Rhodesian government responded by creating protected villages, called Keeps, fenced and guarded villages to stop the villagers from feeding the 'terrorists,' the ZANLA forces. The villagers lived under a 6pm curfew and had to show an ID to leave or return to the protected village before the curfew. One could easily be shot and killed if they didn't produce the ID. They would be suspected of being 'terrorists.' The Ian Smith government didn't want the 'terrorists' getting supplies from villagers.'

'How long did your Sekuru live in these protected villages?'

'Two years.'

'How did he join the war?'

'Sekuru Lovemore was tortured by the Rhodesian forces when a sellout snitched that he was still collaborating with the 'terrorists', the freedom fighters, as a *Mujibha*. After the torture, he fled with his family to our home in Sinoia, present day Chinhoyi.'

'Why did they flee to Sinoia?'

'The cities and towns were safer than rural villages and were a refuge for displaced rural families.'

'What was your relationship with your Sekuru Lovemore like?'

'I loved him a lot. He was in his late teens. He loved to tell stories; folk tales, *Ngano* and other stories about living in the protected villages. He had seen villages bombed and razed to the ground, villagers killed, and dead combatants displayed in public to scare villagers from joining the terrorists. He produced model cars out of wire. I loved driving my wire model car on the dusty streets of the high-density township of Chitambo in Chinhoyi.

Many times, Sekuru Lovemore carried me on his back, and we went to the shops. He also liked courting girls. My dad then owned a small grocery shop and was generous to his in-laws who were suffering from post-traumatic stress disorder.'

'Then what happened next?'

'Unbeknown to my family, Sekuru Lovemore began sneaking out of the house and hanging out with other teenagers at a certain house in Chitambo township. Black townships were recruitment centres for the freedom fighters.'

'Oh no!'

'Sekuru Lovemore was radicalised to join ZANLA and take up arms to fight the Ian Smith regime. Suddenly he was noticeably quiet and was no longer as friendly. He no longer talked about girls. I wanted to ask what the matter was, but he had withdrawn into himself. One day, I followed him from a distance. I saw him shake hands with strange looking youths of his age and he disappeared behind a certain house. I wanted to call him back. I wish to this day that I should have told my mother what Sekuru Lovemore was up to.'

'The following day, Sekuru Lovemore took me to the shops as usual. He bought me a candy cake. He told me that he loved me a lot. He put a letter in my hip pocket and told me to give it to my mother in the evening. He told me he was going somewhere, and he would be back soon. He left me by the gate and walked away. That was the last time I saw my dear Sekuru Lovemore.'

Tears streamed out of Moses' eyes.

'Later in the evening, my worried mother asked me if I knew where Sekuru Lovemore was. I said no. My mum went out looking for him in the houses of some of his friends in the township. She was distraught when she returned home and there was no sign of him. He was always home on time. Late at night I remembered the letter that he had put in my back pocket.'

Moses took out a discoloured envelope and handed the worn-out letter to Tererai. 'This is the letter Sekuru Lovemore wrote to my mum, 47 years ago.'

The letter, which was barely legible, read:

Dear Tete and family

I have decided to join the war of liberation and fight for the freedom of my black people. I have observed the way black people have been oppressed under the Smith regime. I hated living in the protected village, Keep, like an animal in my own ancestral land.

I couldn't just hide from the war in the sanctuary of the towns and cities. I made up my mind to fight for freedom. If it is God's wish that we should unite one day, in an independent country, so be it. But if I should die fighting to liberate my country, please don't mourn me forever. I gave my life for the freedom of future generations. I was not coerced into joining the war of liberation. I joined out of my free will. I joined fellow comrades to free our mother land, Zimbabwe.

I will always love you. Pass my warm regards to little Moses.

I will always love you,

Lovemore.

Moses wiped away tears. 'My mother and the whole family cried for days and wished they had known what Sekuru Lovemore was up to and stopped him. But there was nothing we could do. He had crossed the rubicon. Many youths were recruited by ZANLA that way. The family at the home where Sekuru Lovemore went said they had never seen him. I am sure they knew all about him, but they didn't want to admit it. It was an offence to not report that a family member had joined the war of liberation. The BSAP would have visited our home and arrested my parents. Everyone kept silent those days. You didn't know if your neighbour was a sellout.'

'Did he return from the war?'

'It's a long story. After the ceasefire and the ongoing Lancaster House talks, the combatants left the battlefield for the assembly points.

It was a time of joy and sorrow. Families reunited with their loved ones who had been fighting in the bush. Some members grieved their loved ones that they had lost in the war. The assembly points were dangerous places where the war-hardened combatants were suspicious of the ongoing talks and were itching to return to the bush to fight.

My mum and her brother, Sekuru Chirenje, Sekuru Lovemore's father, visited different assembly points. They returned frustrated that they didn't see Sekuru Lovemore. They held onto the thread of hope that one day Sekuru Lovemore would walk back home. They asked everywhere but none of the combatants remembered Sekuru Lovemore. The hope of finding him alive faded every day. He didn't return home but my family wanted closure.'

'So, what happened then?'

Moses looked up in the sky and sobbed. He avoided eye contact with Tererai.

Then he continued, 'Then in 1981 a disabled stranger with crutches walked into the yard of our home, in Chinhoyi. At first, I thought it was Sekuru Lovemore but realised that this man looked older and shorter. I was disappointed. The stranger introduced himself to my mother and father as the commander of the section that Sekuru Lovemore and other combatants belonged to. He described Sekuru Lovemore as a brave freedom fighter. He narrated the tragic story of the section that he commanded.'

***

The ZANLA freedom fighters had regularly raided remote grocery shops and looted food, clothes, and other provisions. But on one fateful day, they raided a white owned rural grocery store.

But unbeknown to them there was an observation point of Rhodesian forces on top of a nearby mountain. The observers had spotted them and radioed in a request for back up. The back-up had responded quickly.

On the way out of the grocery shop with loot, the comrades were fired at from helicopters and quickly surrounded by ground troops parachuting from helicopters. There was gunfire. The comrades were outnumbered and outgunned.

Five of the nine comrades were killed on the scene. Sekuru Lovemore had survived the shooting. He and three of his comrades were captured and taken away.

It was the routine for the triumphant Rhodesian forces to display the dead bodies of the comrades to warn the villagers that such fate would befall them if they joined the 'terrorists.' None of the villagers knew where the dead bodies were buried.

Sekuru Lovemore was taken to hospital for treatment. He was guarded on his hospital bed.

After Sekuru Lovemore got better, he was taken to a detention camp where he was tortured for information. His interrogators wanted to know where the freedom fighters' bases were located, the weapons they had in their arsenal, their operations, their military tactics and how they received provisions from outside the country.

But Sekuru Lovemore refused to talk and sell out his comrades. They continued to torture him and tried to turn him. He saw the section commander during the torture. He told him about his torture. He gave him my mum's address in Sinoia. Sekuru Lovemore had died during the torture and his body was dumped at an unknown location.

The section commander had feigned cooperation with the Rhodesian forces. He miraculously escaped captivity and rejoined the comrades. The other two comrades died during torture. He had expected to reunite with Sekuru Lovemore at the nearby assembly point after the ceasefire. But they didn't meet. He said that Sekuru Lovemore was a gallant freedom fighter.

My mum broke down and cried. I went inside the house, now filled with wailing. It was a bittersweet closure for the family.

Weeks later, my family went to our rural village to conduct the Shona cultural traditions and rituals to bring Sekuru Lovemore's 'wandering spirit back home.'

According to Shona tradition, Sekuru Lovemore's spirit was wandering far away from home. It needed to be brought back home and appeased. A grave for Sekuru Lovemore was erected in his village.'

***

'I am really sorry to hear about the tragic story of your Sekuru Lovemore. Your story has given a new meaning to the Tomb of the Unknown Soldier. It has given a face to the unknown soldier.'

'The tomb pays homage to the gallant freedom fighters, dead and alive, including my Sekuru Lovemore, who paid the ultimate sacrifice to liberate this country.'

'Fair enough. I respect the ultimate sacrifices that your Sekuru Lovemore and many more freedom fighters made to free this country. But look at the current state of the country; high level of corruption, the high unemployment, the brain drain, the suppression of freedom of speech, and incarceration without trial of opposition party members like Sikhala, the looting of the nation's resources shown in the Gold Mafia documentary and many more problems bedevilling the country.'

'It is clear that the country is facing challenges that have also been worsened by the sanctions that have affected economic development. But what has this to do with my dead Sekuru Lovemore?'

'Sekuru Lovemore and other freedom fighters fought for freedom. But we are not eating the fruits of that freedom. Look, I have a BA degree in Shona, but I work here at the Heroes Acre as a gardener and general hand. Don't I deserve a chance to get a good job, without paying someone corrupt to get employment? Didn't your Sekuru Lovemore and others die so that we could live in a country full of milk and honey?'

'Yes. I have sympathy for you, Tererai, for the problems you are experiencing in the country. I don't have a right to lecture you on who you should vote for in the upcoming elections, when I live in the diaspora. Your choice is your constitutional right.'

'I won't vote for these corrupt leaders. I will vote for change. It is high time there was change in this country.'

'You are entitled to hold your opinion and vote for anyone who you think brings the change you want. But that doesn't take away the fact that my Sekuru Lovemore and other gallant fighters, immortalised by this Tomb of the Unknown Soldier, died so that you could exercise your constitutional right. It is up to you, whether you want to vote to safeguard those sacrifices and gains of liberation or as you say, you want to vote for change.'

'I will definitely vote for change.'

'Good day, and good luck, Tererai.'

He watched Moses walk away. He felt sympathy for him. He lived in the diaspora but carried the deep scars from a past, long forgotten war. Maybe Moses was right that the younger generation must not take for granted the hard-won gains of independence. But what was there to celebrate in this wasteland? The future looked bleak for him. His dreams were deferred.

Tererai thought that Moses' Sekuru Lovemore might have been an old man with children and grandchildren by now. He felt Moses' pain.

Tererai realised that every generation struggles with its own problems. The previous generation fought hard for independence. But his generation was fighting a different struggle against the liberators for a better future.

All he wanted was to enter the voting booth and vote for change and the future he hoped for. But would the change that he craved for materialise? He wasn't sure. At least he had a better understanding of why other people still voted for the ruling party, despite and still, the problems bedevilling the country. Tererai returned to his weeding. He was lost in thought.

Dark and Lovely

Viola noticed that she stood out in a crowd, in Bexhill-on-sea, because of her uniquely darker skin colour. White people in shops and streets stared at her pitch-black complexion.

She disliked the gazes and looked away, feeling uncomfortable. Now she was more self-conscious about her skin complexion than when she lived in Harare.

'Why do white people stare at me like that, mum?' she paused, munching the roast potatoes and chicken on her dinner plate.

'I don't know why they stare at all of us in that funny way. Maybe because they didn't grow up among black people with darker skin like you and me. So, naturally, they are curious when they meet you on the street. I don't know.'

Viola sighed. 'I don't like being stared at like I am a gorilla.'

'But who says you are? It's just your own negative perception. I had the same negative self-image when I moved over here. I felt violated every time someone stared at me in public. But with time, I got used to the stares and bland smiles when our eyes met. I got on with my life. You will get used to the gazes of white people.'

'Can I tell them to stop staring at me?'

'No. Don't say that. It will cause offence. Do not stare back either. That is rude.'

Viola shook her head. 'I do not understand this, mum; they can stare at me, but I can't stare back at them, nor can I tell them to stop staring at me, because apparently, according to you, that is rude behaviour and causes offence?'

'You must always respect other people.'

'Even when they stare at me like I am a gorilla? I don't understand.' Viola threw her hands in the air, in resignation and shook her head.

'You will get more funnier stares when you start Sixth Form College soon.'

***

On the first day in Sixth Form College, Viola noticed how the white English Literature Teacher stopped typing on her laptop and stared at her as she walked into the classroom. Viola immediately looked away and sat at the back of the classroom.

The teacher stole glances at Viola during the lesson on Merchant of Venice.

Viola looked down and started sketching an image of the teacher staring at her, in her notebook.

The chime of the bell at the end of the lesson brought relief to Viola. She quickly gathered her books, shoved them in her handbag and dashed out of the classroom without muttering a word to the teacher.

In the college canteen, Viola ordered a beef burger with lettuce, ketch up, cheddar cheese, slices of pickles and onions, served with fluffy, crisp chips. She sat alone at the far end of a long, white table. She munched the burger and chips and read the latest online news stories from the New Zimbabwe portal. Occasionally, she lifted her head and glanced around the canteen.

Other students sat at different tables, in small groups. Viola couldn't be bothered about them. She was in no mood to talk to anyone. She yawned and missed her girlfriends back in Harare. She wished they were here for hearty girly gossip and laughter.

Viola daydreamed in the History class. She just did not like the lanky, snobbish white teacher with spectacles. He was so full of himself. She gazed at the clock till the end of the dreary lesson.

***

'How was college today?' mum asked her at dinner.

'Boring. The English Teacher kept staring at me like she had seen Kunta Kinte from the film, *Roots*. The History Teacher was boring and snobbish. My mind wandered off most of the time.'

'Now, listen to me, young lady; stop that belligerent behaviour. You must respect your teachers and concentrate on your lessons. I am sending you to college to learn, not to disrespect your teachers. Do you hear me loud and clear?' Mum was panting like a greyhound.

'Yes, mum.' Viola nodded.

'Did you make new friends today?'

'No.'

'Why not?'

'The other students ignored me.'

'Make an effort to befriend them.'

'What if they don't want to hang out with me?'

'At least try to befriend someone tomorrow. You need new friends in the new college.'

***

The following day, Viola sat next to a white student in the canteen. He had frizzled hair and dressed like a geek with thick-lensed spectacles.

'Hi,' Viola muttered to him.

The geek gazed at her without uttering a word. He looked away and continued eating his bread and soup.

Viola felt stupid and snubbed.

She avoided eye contact with him. The geek occasionally stole glances at her like she was a phantom. He stood up with his food tray and walked over to a group of boys.

Viola continued eating her chips. Then she overheard the geek mutter the word, 'Lupita.'

The other boys at the table burst out laughing.

Viola almost choked on her chips with anger. She finished eating and bolted out of the canteen.

***

On the way home Viola called on Millie, her mum's best friend, a hairdresser at Fragrant hair salon.

'You don't look like a happy bunny. What is the matter, Viola?' Millie asked. 'How is college?'

Viola frowned.

Millie put her hand on her shoulder. 'Now, tell me, what's the matter?'

'I tried making friends with this white student and he snubbed me. He poked fun at my darker skin colour with his mates. He muttered that I looked like Lupita Nyong'o, that darker-skinned Black Hollywood actor. His mates burst out laughing at that. I wanted to go and punch him in the face. I was seething with rage.'

'Oh, no. That was so unkind. Obviously, the student had a prejudice against your darker skin. It is called colourism. But do not despair, girl. I have a beauty secret, a cream that lightens your skin.'

'Does it really work?'

'Yes. It works wonders on your skin.'

Millie took the tube of cream from the display shelf. She smiled and waved the tube in Viola's face. 'This only costs five pounds.'

Viola bought the cream and rushed home to try it on her face. She was happy that she had the cream that would lighten her skin.

Before bed, Viola went to the bathroom. She glanced at her image in the mirror like Narcissus. She rubbed the cream over her face. The cream was light textured and left her skin feeling comfortable and visibly well-balanced. She liked it.

***

The following day Viola returned home from college, and she found mum sitting on her bed, in her bedroom.

'What is this?' Mum raised her voice, visibly angry and waving the tube of skin cream.

'Skin cream.' Viola cringed.

'I know it is skin cream. Why are you bleaching your skin? Are you out of your mind?'

'I am being bullied at college about my darker skin. So, I wanted to lighten my skin.'

'It is not right that you are being bullied about your darker skin. But you must not use this cheap skin lightening cream.'

'Why not?'

'There is mercury and hydroquinone in this cream. Prolonged use of this cream can lead to skin damage, poisoning, and cancer, and even liver and kidney malfunction.'

'But I don't intend to use this cream for long, mum. Just till my skin looks lighter.'

'Why don't you take pride in the natural beauty of your skin, your God-given skin? Ever heard of the "Black is beautiful" slogan?'

'No.'

'African Americans coined this phrase in the 1960s to promote pride in the black skin. The slogan dispelled dominant, white racist prejudices and myths at the time; that natural features of black people such as skin colour, facial features and hair were apparently ugly.'

'I see. But that was then.'

'Ever heard of the Looking Glass Self?'

'What is that?'

'Cooley, a sociologist, said a person forms their self-esteem and subjectivity based on how they think others perceive them. If you think others view you as ugly, then you see ugliness in the looking glass. You must develop a positive self-image.'

'How am I going to do that?'

'You need self-love. Stop using skin lightening cream and embrace your darker skin, your perfect imperfections.

Embrace other black women with dark skin like Lupita and your name's sake, Viola Davis. Believe that black is beautiful. Beauty comes from within, love.'

'I don't understand what the fuss is, mum.'

'One day, you will understand.' Mum left Viola's bedroom with the tube of cream.

Viola was unhappy that mum had taken away the cream. But she didn't want to continue arguing with her. Mum had temper tantrums.

***

Meanwhile at college, Viola continued to be subjected to more bullying by the geek and his friends. She was afraid of reporting the bullying incidents to the teachers. So, she avoided going to the canteen at the same time as those boys.

Viola returned to Fragrant Hair Salon to see Milly. She was busy with a client, so she waited until she had finished with the client.

'Did the cream work wonders on your skin?' Milly asked, gazing at Viola's face.

'No. Unfortunately, mum took away the cream and destroyed it. She lectured me not to use cheap cream from China containing chemicals that could apparently cause skin cancer. But I won't listen to her. Can you please sell me another tube?'

'You must listen to your mum's advice.'

'No. I am a grown-up girl. I know what I want. Mum does not listen to me. She treats me like a toddler. She is always preaching like Joyce Meyer.'

'If you insist, I will sell you a different cream. I have run out of stock of the cream I sold you last time. Try out this new one. It is just as good.' Milly handed her the new cream.

Viola paid for it and went home. She hid the cream under the mattress where mum would not look.

At bedtime, Viola took out the cream and went to the bathroom. She rubbed the cream over her face and modelled in front of the mirror. She was happy that she had another skin lightening cream and had outwitted mum.

***

When Viola woke up the following morning, her face felt dry and itchy. She touched it gently. Her skin felt cracked and sore. She rushed to the bathroom and gazed in the mirror. Eczema had developed all over her face.

She wouldn't dare tell mum about the Eczema, lest she should scream at her, 'I told you so, but you didn't listen.' She dared not go to college looking like a zombie from Dawn of the Dead. The college bullies would have a field day. She returned to her bedroom and jumped into bed. She pulled the duvet over her head.

When Viola heard mum plodding towards her bedroom, she froze. Mum opened the door. 'Why are you not dressed for college?'

'I have severe diarrhoea. I am not going to college today,' she said, still hiding her face under the duvet.

'Alright, then. Mind what you eat. Take some Imodium from the medicine drawer. I will see you in the evening. I hope you will be feeling better then. I love you, sweetheart. I must go. I might be late for a morning meeting.'

When the drone of mum's car faded away in the distance, Viola jumped out of bed and straightened her floral night dress. She sauntered to the bathroom. She gazed in the mirror. She massaged her itchy, cracked, and sore skin. She took out a tube of E45 cream from the bathroom cupboard. She scooped cream onto her palms and rubbed the cream gently over the skin.

Viola went to the kitchen and made a bowl of corn flakes and a cup of tea. She went to the lounge and perched on the sofa. She hunched her shoulders and sighed.

On Sky TV news, the Russians were bombing civilians in Mariupol. She hated bullies like Putin.

She scrolled to the YouTube app and typed in the search word, 'Colourism.' Many videos popped up, including ones with black female celebrities like Beyonce and Rihanna, talking frankly about their experiences of colourism. She scrolled down the list of videos. Then she clicked on the video; *People of Colour discuss the impact of Colourism* by Good Morning America.

The video chronicled how colourism originated in slavery and colonialism, how women with lighter skin received higher wages than darker skinned women, and how colourism is believed to cause long term mental and physical trauma on victims.

Viola paused the video and munched corn flakes, then she sipped tea. She resumed playing the video. An organisation, *Beauty Well Project*, raised awareness of the impact of colourism and advocated empowerment and representation of darker skinned women in professions like journalism and mentoring by black role models.

Towards the end of the video, Viola felt sad that most of the black women saw themselves as victims of colourism. She didn't want to view herself as a victim. She wanted to feel good, and live comfortable in her darker skin. But she didn't know how to do that.

Suddenly a perfume advert, Daisy by Marc Jacobs started playing. Three models, two white girls and one black girl with dark skin, were dancing in a field of daisies. Viola's attention was captivated by the infectious smile of the black model frolicking in the grass with confidence.

Suddenly, Viola realised that she lacked the infectious smile and the self-confidence of the black model. She decided to take up modelling classes to improve her self-confidence and dressing style. She realised that she didn't necessarily need the skin lightening cream after all.

Maybe mum was right, that black is beautiful. She resolved to love her natural black skin.

Then Viola remembered that she had to lie to mum that she was feeling better when she returned from work. She wondered how to explain the eczema on her face. She would say, with a straight face, that she had an allergic reaction to the bath soak foam. That was a plausible explanation. Viola rolled her big eyes.

A Sobering Encounter

I stopped my car by the roadside and kept the engine running. A police patrol car pulled up behind me. The full beam of headlights and flashing sirens in the dark night blinded me.

My breath reeked of wine. My heart pounded as two white police officers got out of the patrol car. I shoved peppermint gum in my mouth and chewed it like a cow chewing grass. Balls of sweat formed on my forehead as the officers approached me.

'Sir, can I please see your driver's licence?' One officer shone a torch into my eyes. I looked ahead and handed him my driver's licence.

'Sir, are you the registered keeper of this vehicle?'

'Yes.'

'Can I please see your vehicle registration book?'

'I don't have it now.'

'Where is it?'

'Home.'

'Do you have any other proof of ownership?'

'No.'

'Sir, does this car belong to you?'

'Yes. Check the DVLA database.' I cleared my throat.

'How did you afford this car?'

'I beg your pardon! Are you implying that a black man like me can't afford to buy a brand-new BMW X5?'

'No, sir.'

'So, what are you implying?' I frowned.

'There've been several carjackings of expensive cars in London recently.'

'So, you stopped me because you suspected that I am a car carjacker?'

'No, sir. It is just a routine stop.'

'I don't think so. Please, officer, don't racially profile me. I'm a professional footballer, not a carjacker.'

'Which league do you play for?'

'English Premier League.'

The police officer glared at me. I looked down. Then he looked around the vehicle.

'I will run a quick DVLA vehicle registration check now.' The officer returned to the patrol car. The other police officer remained behind, eyeing me suspiciously. I chewed more gum.

Moments later, the officer, my interrogator, returned. 'Everything checked out fine. Safe journey, Sir.' He handed back my driver's licence.

'I told you this is my car, officer.'

'No offence intended. Just doing my job.' The police officer checked his watch.

'Good night, sir,' the other police officer spoke for the first time.

'Good night, officers.'

The officers walked back to their patrol car.

For a moment, I was upset about how the police officer had racially profiled me. I was a law-abiding citizen, most of the time. I exhaled. The fresh peppermint smell of chewing gum masked the stench of wine under my breath.

I wondered what would have happened if the officers had smelled a rat and done a breathalyser test on me. I sighed and immediately felt sober as the police patrol car sped off.

Keep on Trying

Vimbai wandered like a zombie around Bexhill Town Centre. Floods of tears streamed down her cheeks. She took out a tissue from her handbag and wiped away the tears. She sniffled and blew her nose into the tissue.

Then she perched on a wooden bench in the sweltering summer sun. She peered into the clear blue sky. 'Lord, why me?' She muttered and sighed. Her eyes tilted like a camera from the sky to the bold sign: **Oxfam Charity Shop**. She was in a dreamlike state.

She stood up and pottered into the charity shop, in a daze. She was the only customer inside the well-stocked shop with women's and men's wear, books, and gifts. A strong lavender scent hit her nostrils. A shop worker, a middle-aged white woman, behind the counter smiled at Vimbai. But she ignored her friendly smile and she looked away. Vimbai examined the dresses and outfits in the women's wear section. She took two dresses off the hangers and felt the soft texture of the fabrics. She stole another glance at the shop worker. Their eyes met again. Vimbai feigned a smile.

'All these clothes are half price,' said the shop worker walking over to Vimbai. 'Today is your lucky day. Nice matching outfits.' Her wide smile could disarm a thief. 'Do you want some help choosing outfits?'

'No, thank you.'

The shop worker walked back to the counter.

Vimbai put back the clothes and finally settled on a floral skirt and matching blouse. She disappeared behind the curtains of the changing room. She glanced in the mirror, at her small, soft tummy. She sat down on a stool and dropped the clothes on the floor. She cupped her face in her hands and sobbed.

'Are you alright, in there, darling?'

'Yes, I'm fine.' Vimbai jolted back to reality. She wiped away the tears and quickly tried on the skirt and blouse.

'Did the clothes fit well?'

'Yes.' Vimbai parted the curtains of the changing room and walked out. She avoided eye contact with the shop worker.

'You took 15 minutes in there and I thought you'd had a seizure. Are you alright, darling?' Vimbai began to sob uncontrollably.

'What is the matter, darling?' The shop worker drew closer to her and touched her on the shoulder. Vimbai continued to sob. There was momentary silence.

'Did I say something to upset you?'

'No.' Vimbai shook her head.

'So, what's the matter?'

'I just had a miscarriage, and I am heartbroken.'

'Oh, no!' The shop worker hugged Vimbai and caressed her on the head. 'I am so sorry, poppet.'

***

Vimbai and Dambudzo, her husband, had been trying for a baby for a year. One evening, Vimbai went to the toilet and carried out a pregnancy test. 'We are going to have a baby!' She screamed, bolting out of the toilet, and running towards

Dambudzo in the lounge. She showed him the double lines on the pregnancy test kit.

Dambudzo stood up from the couch and looked at the pregnancy test kit 'Yes, yes.' He couldn't contain his joy.

They danced around the lounge like party kids.

'The heavens have finally answered our prayers,' said Dambudzo, looking upwards and lifting his hands up like a devout worshipper. 'Thank you, lord.'

Finally, Vimbai was elated to be on the road to motherhood, after four pregnancy tests.

'Gosh, we have a lot to do from now until childbirth. Should we tell the family?'

'No, no. Not yet, we might jinx it. But the choice is yours. You are the mother-to-be. I will support any decision you make.'

'I think we should tell them after the first scan because we need them for emotional support during the pregnancy.' Vimbai fist pumped.

'Fine, mother of my baby,' Dambudzo smiled. 'We need to buy the baby's clothes from catalogues, choose a good Shona name and research nurseries.'

'Not so fast dad-to-be.'

Daily, Vimbai began to see the signs of pregnancy and feel her body change. She experienced tiredness and struggled to keep her eyes open at work. She had poor concentration during exam revision at home. She changed her work out routine to ease the strain on her body. She loved to constantly remind herself that she was a mother-to-be.

Then Vimbai experienced some bleeding in week six. She panicked and told Dambudzo. They researched online and discovered that implantation bleeding was a potential sign of a miscarriage. Vimbai couldn't sit still, and she constantly caressed her belly.

'Stop worrying, darling. A miscarriage won't happen to you. Stop panicking, that may affect the growth of the baby. Besides, you haven't had any prenatal tests to confirm that something is wrong.'

'Don't you dare tell me to stop worrying. Every woman worries about the child she is carrying in her womb. Clueless, bloody men!'

'Sorry, Vimbai, I rest my case.'

Three days later, Vimbai had further bleeding. She phoned her GP surgery. The GP referred her to the Early Pregnancy Unit where she had her first scan. The baby, at seven weeks, was so tiny, with a faint heartbeat.

'Many pregnant women experience bleeding during pregnancy,' the doctor said, adjusting his spectacles. 'But your scans show that the baby is fine.'

'Thank you, doctor. Thank you very much.' Vimbai felt like a weight had been lifted off her chest.

Vimbai and Dambudzo jumped around, hugged, and kissed as they strolled out of the Early Pregnancy Unit clutching the huge brown envelope with the first pregnancy scan.

Vimbai thought this was the right time to share the good news with their close family. She messaged them. Her phone pinged with messages of joy and best wishes.

In week eight, Vimbai felt better and shared daily pregnancy updates with the family. It felt right to do so.

In week ten, she had a midwife appointment. Vimbai was excited and also anxious. The midwife weighed her, worked out her BMI, and asked all the routine prenatal questions. She reassured Vimbai that the baby was developing as expected and she was at a low risk of miscarriage. Afterwards, Vimbai toasted to the positive news with Baileys in the lounge with Dambudzo.

Days before her week 12 scan Vimbai experienced another implantation bleeding. She was worried and told Dambudzo. He rushed her back to the Early Pregnancy Unit. Family members texted Vimbai when she didn't text the daily updates. She texted back reassuring them that she was on a routine hospital scan. She had good luck messages.

Vimbai and Dambudzo entered the sonographer's room. The sonographer, an Asian man, applied gel over Vimbai's bulging belly. He placed a small handheld probe on her skin and moved it over her tummy. He looked at the monitor as he moved the probe.

Vimbai shifted with the cold sensation of the gel and the probe moving on her tummy.

Then everything went wrong. The sonographer gazed long and hard at the screen monitor.

Vimbai glared at the screen and felt something wasn't right. The baby looked much smaller.

'I am afraid the probe isn't picking up the ultrasound. In other words, there is no heartbeat from the foetus,' said the sonographer.

'What do you mean there is no heartbeat?' Vimbai looked askance at him.

'I am so sorry; this is a sign that you had a miscarriage.'

'What miscarriage are you talking about?' Dambudzo glared at the sonographer and then at the monitor. Shock was etched on his face.

'I am so sorry.'

Vimbai and Dambudzo sat quiet in disbelief. She felt like someone had punctured a hole through her chest and ripped out her heart.

Instinctively, they started sobbing in each other's arms. This wasn't how it was meant to end. *Lord, no!*

On the way home Vimbai sat in the passenger's seat numb as a widow, sobbing all the way.

At home, sitting on the couch, Dambudzo's arm around her, Vimbai continued sobbing and sniffling. Hours went by. She knew their family was starting to get worried. They had been patiently waiting for an update. She couldn't muster the courage to text them, so she asked Dambudzo to break the sad news of the miscarriage, a few weeks after breaking the good news of the pregnancy.

She wondered if she had jinxed it by telling the family about the pregnancy before 12 weeks. Should she have kept quiet?

The following days were dark. Vimbai and Dambudzo were mentally and emotionally drained. The outpouring of emotional support from family soothed the gaping wounds. It was comforting to know that they had a strong, supportive family network that shared in their pain. Their small flat turned into a florist's shop.

***

'I'm so sorry, love, about your miscarriage,' said the charity shop worker with a face contorted with sympathy.

'Thank you.' Vimbai wiped away tears.

'Thank God your family lives close to you, here in England, and they were supportive.'

'Yes. My parents emigrated from Rhodesia, present day Zimbabwe, to England in the 1970s during the Rhodesian bush war. I was born and bred in London.'

'I see. It is understandable how you are grieving your loss. Women deal with miscarriage in different ways.'

'I am heartbroken and confused. I don't know how to make sense of this pain.'

'I understand your pain, poppet.'

'I don't know how I can move on after this heartbreak. My dreams of motherhood are deferred.'

'You can move on beyond the pain and grief, love. Wounds heal with time.'

'How can I heal? When I feel like such a failure. When I feel like the miscarriage was all my fault.'

'It's not your fault, love. I see you are overwhelmed by guilt and self-blame.'

The shop worker held Vimbai's hands. 'I felt the same way too when I had two miscarriages before having my son who is now twenty-five years old.' Tears sparkled in her eyes.

There was momentary silence, a woman-to-woman processing of shared grief and pain.

'But life goes on, poppet. You can't mourn forever; you must move on. I mourned the two miscarriages. But I kept the faith and kept trying for another baby. I was third time lucky. Keep the faith, love, don't give up. Keep on trying.'

The shop worker hugged her. There was silence. Vimbai sobbed on her shoulder. The woman caressed her on the back like a baby to calm her.

'You did the right thing to share your pain with your family. Miscarriage is a common occurrence among pregnant women. It's also a taboo subject among some women. They hide their grief from family and friends and suffer in silence.'

'How did your family and friends help you through the pain of the two-miscarriages?'

'They validated my pain and grief. They were a secure network of love, compassion and understanding during the grieving process.'

'You're right. I received a lot of flowers and postcards from my family. My brother and sister-in-law sent me a large bouquet of white roses after I messaged them about the heartbreaking news. My brother, a police officer, wrote on the card, *"Thinking of you and Dambudzo, at this difficult moment, from the London Metropolitan police."*

'That was so kind of them. You need family like that, in such painful times.'

'I can't believe that last week I was 11 weeks pregnant, full of joy and hope for the baby growing inside my womb. But now, I am sad, hopeless, and grieving.'

'I am so sorry for your loss, poppet.'

'Thank you so much for your kind words. I feel much better than when I walked in here. You've lifted the dark cloud that was hanging over my mind.' Vimbai smiled. 'What is your name by the way?'

'Sue. You are welcome, love. Best wishes with trying for another baby.'

Vimbai left the charity shop that afternoon thanking Sue, the charity shop worker for her empathy. She had soothed her gaping wound of pain, sadness, guilt, and self-blame. She covered her with a warm blanket of compassion.

Vimbai realised that she wasn't alone, not the first woman to have a miscarriage. She remembered Sue's kind and sincere words, 'Keep on trying.' Vimbai felt a certain peace that she couldn't understand. Her pain and grief was gone. It was replaced by hope, a hope of motherhood.

Maybe her Good Lord had answered her prayer for comforting and sent Sue. The comfort of a stranger. Sue was at the right place and at the right time. Vimbai remembered the words, 'The Lord works in mysterious ways.' *Was this one of the Lord's mysterious ways? Lord knows.* She smiled.

Behind the Façade – a novella

Part One

1

Rose perched on a comfortable seat inside Paradise Life Ministries Pentecostal Church and gazed around the former cinema hall transformed into a church. Well-dressed men, women and children worshipped their God with fire in their souls.

A fresh breeze diffused inside the church auditorium on that hot mid-August morning.

A handsome young man took to the podium and led the singing of a melodious praise and worship song. Rose's eyes transfixed on the man. She was instantly seduced by the smoothness of his singing voice, his shiny, black designer suit, and his confidence. He exuded deep spirituality. He must have been just about the same age as her, twenty-five.

Rose wondered what it would feel like to be this man's girlfriend. *Any woman would die to date this handsome man,* she thought. She imagined strolling in the park, arm in arm with him, and being kissed on the cheek. She smiled. She jolted back to reality. She felt a guilty conscience for thinking such unclean thoughts inside the church during a service! It was her first time to attend church here.

Then a charismatic, middle-aged man dressed in an expensive white three-piece suit, came onto the podium. The church exploded into a frenzy of cheers. 'Can all the first-time visitors please stand up? I am Pastor Nehemiah Gumbo, the Senior Pastor, and Founder of Paradise Life Ministries Pentecostal Church.'

Rose and a dozen others stood up.

Pastor Nehemiah surveyed the visitors with his deep searching eyes. 'Welcome to our church.' He turned to the church, 'Let us give our visitors a warm Christian welcome.' There was rapturous clapping.

Pastor Nehemiah started preaching on the parable of the talents. His sermon was measured, exciting and full of anecdotes. His preaching didn't appear crass nor insult the intelligence of the congregants. He beseeched the believers to invest in their talents before the master returns. His charisma aroused loyalty among the frenzied believers. He wiped off balls of sweat from his face with a handkerchief.

Rose loved the sermon that was a mixture of prosperity gospel, human potential, positive thinking, and seasoned with bible scriptures.

A short stout woman who appeared to be Pastor Nehemiah's wife, sitting in the front row, shouted, 'Amen' after every important anecdote.

'Poor, loyal Pastor's wife,' Rose thought. She instantly disliked her exaggerated piety, typical of pastor's wives. She wondered what she really was like at home with her family, away from the service where she was drunk with religious opium of the mind.

Pastor Nehemiah constantly gazed at Rose like a lovelorn teenager at the prom.

Rose looked down or away when their eyes met. His eyes focused on her like a searchlight. This unhinged her.

After the sermon, Pastor Nehemiah made an altar call and beseeched the sinners to come forward and repent. The sheep, plagued by a guilty conscience, flocked to the altar for deliverance. The pastor laid his hands on the repentant sinners and prayed for God's healing and deliverance.

There were wild cheers when the sinners fell down on the carpet and convulsed in fits of demonic manifestations, and they were later healed.

Rose was mystified by the charade and 'performance' of laying hands, demonic manifestations, and instant healing.

The praise and worship team began singing a low tune as the sinners were being delivered by the laying of hands, 'in the name of Jesus.'

Then the singing suddenly stopped. Pastor Nehemiah led a prayer for 'the delivered sheep' to continue following the good shepherd, Jesus Christ.

Then Pastor Nehemiah beseeched the faithful congregants to give their tithes and offerings to the House of the Lord.

The congregants deposited envelopes of tithes and offerings into boxes that ushers passed around the pews.

After the service, Pastor Nehemiah met and greeted the first-time visitors to Paradise Life Church. He tickled Rose in the palm. 'Thank you for visiting Paradise Life Ministries Church. What's your name?'

'Rose Moyo. That was an excellent sermon,' Rose lied with a straight face. In fact, the sermon was good but not excellent.

'Thank you.'

'The praise and worship team did an excellent job too. What is the name of the praise and worship leader?'

'Oh, that's Brother Kudakwashe. He is blessed with a good singing voice.'

Pastor Nehemiah winked at Rose and handed her his business card. 'Please call me,' he whispered into her ear and peered at her cleavage.

Rose felt uncomfortable. *Why were his leering eyes peeking at her cleavage? Why did a married pastor give her his business card when they had just met?* Rose feigned a smile.

Pastor Nehemiah introduced Brother Kudakwashe to Rose.

'That was a good praise and worship session,' Rose shook Kudakwashe's hand.

'All credit belongs to the Jehovah above, who blessed me with the voice of worship.'

Pastor Nehemiah moved on and greeted other visitors to the church.

'Can you sing, Rose? You can come and join our Tuesday night choir practice,' Brother Kudakwashe was grinning. Rose grinned at him too. There was apparent chemistry between them.

'I can sing but not as well as you. I will think about it.' A wider grin punctuated Rose's face.

'We always welcome new members to the choir,' Brother Kudakwashe said. 'I look forward to seeing you at the choir practice.'

'I will definitely think about that.' Rose tried to musk the joy that was bubbling inside her heart.

'No need to think about it. Just show up for a few practice sessions and see how you like it. Then make up your mind whether to join us.'

'Thank you, Brother Kudakwashe. My pleasure to meet you,' Rose smiled like she had known Kudakwashe for a long time.

'Nice meeting you too, Rose. Hope to see you again on Tuesday night,' said Brother Kudakwashe, shaking her hand.

Rose greeted other congregants and was delighted by the warmth of the congregation at Paradise Life Ministries Pentecostal Church. She had visited other churches in the city of Harare that were less friendly. Here the congregants were polite, welcoming, and respectful.

Rose was happy to join this congregation. She hoped to develop new friendships and, fingers crossed, find a suitable God-fearing man to marry her in the church. *Brother Kudakwashe would be a good catch, she thought.*

Rose liked Pastor Nehemiah's friendly and approachable nature. He appeared caring. She felt happy that she was in the right place and worshipping among the right people.

But she knew that when a rose, her name's sake, was planted in the right soil and right weather conditions, it must bloom among the insects, bees and birds that peck its beautiful petals.

Nevertheless, Rose was baffled by the speaking in tongues, the live band, the teachings on the Holy Spirit, and the paying of tithes and offerings. She had a lot to learn.

***

That afternoon Rose visited her mum in Mufakose. 'Guess what, I attended a service at a new church, Paradise Life Ministries Church in the city centre this morning.'

Mum glared at her. 'Is it one of those Pentecostal churches mushrooming everywhere in the city centre, and led by those money hungry, fake pastors, the charlatans?' Mum shot straight.

'No, mum. Paradise Life Church is different. It is a good church, led by a God-fearing man called Pastor Nehemiah Gumbo.'

'Yeah, right. How do you know that he is really God-fearing when you have just met him?'

'The congregation is so friendly and welcoming.'

'I don't trust these new Pentecostal churches, Rose. Strange things are said to happen there. Remember that time when there was a rumour that some of the churches were practising Satanism?'

'Mum, I am an adult. I can choose the right church to attend.'

'What is the matter with you, Rose, now you don't take my advice? You seem to know it all, at twenty-five years old.' Mum walked over to the chest of drawers and took out a newspaper cutting.

'Read this story. Don't say I didn't warn you about these fake, holier than thou city churches led by charlatans.'

The cutting was a front-page story of a prominent pastor who had been convicted of sexually abusing female congregants, in his church, and was due for sentencing soon.

There was a look of real concern on mum's face.

Rose shrugged. 'Mum, not all city churches are run by charlatans. Paradise Life Ministries Pentecostal Church is a good bible believing church.'

'That is how these city churches lure believers. They appear friendly when you first attend service. They put on this beautiful façade of being a good church. With time the charlatans show their true colours; they suck money out of poor believers with social problems and bamboozle them with their prosperity gospel and sexually abuse young women like you. The pastors can sell ice to the Eskimos. Something sinister and ungodly lurks behind that façade.'

Rose stood up from the sofa and walked over to the window. She peered outside. 'How is your blood pressure this week, mum?'

'My blood pressure has been quite high this week. I just don't feel well. How is work?'

'Work is fine, just busier with the school exams approaching.'

'I have a letter of yours, delivered yesterday.' Mum took the letter out of the drawers and handed it to Rose.

Rose opened the letter. Her heart almost stopped when she realised who had written the letter. It simply read;

Dear Rose,

You and I will get even one day. You thought you were clever and conned me off my money. I will not rest until we get even.

Rodney.

'Who wrote you the letter?'

'It is just one of those companies trying to sell me what I don't want. Shall I start cooking *Sadza*, chicken with stew and green vegetables?' Rose folded the letter and put it in her handbag. She went into the kitchen.

***

Sitting in his study that afternoon, Pastor Nehemiah Gumbo cogitated about Rose. Her beauty had left him mesmerised. He reminisced the first time he had laid his eyes on the beautiful woman who would eventually become his wife, Mai Gumbo. He had the same feeling of being overwhelmed by the lure and scent of a gorgeous woman. His heart was pumping hard and fast.

He tried to get Rose out of his mind. But he failed. In the end, he yearned for her. He loved the thrill of pursuing a pretty woman, and the joy of the conquest.

Then he came back to his senses. He remembered that he was the Senior Pastor of Paradise Life Ministries Church, a husband and father of two teenagers.

Why was he so infatuated by a young woman whom he had just met and laid his eyes on? It was against the teachings of the bible, to lust after another woman, who was not his wife.

It was a fact that his marriage had its challenges. Things were no longer hunky dory in the union. He remembered the old Shona saying, *Chakafukidza dzimba matenga.* Many are the goings on under the roofs of homes.

Pastor Nehemiah loathed the lack of sexual intimacy with his wife, Mai Gumbo. Menopause had robbed him of the beautiful wife he once knew and loved. She had changed.

Mai Gumbo was no longer the obedient woman who stood by every decision that he made. She was now independent-minded. He wondered what had happened to the 'deep respect for the husband.' He gradually began to dislike her quest for independence.

Pastor Nehemiah knew he had changed too. He was always busy growing the church and ministry, and there was less quality time with his family.

The children, Tadiwanashe and Anesu, were now teenagers and they presented a new challenge with the vicissitudes of growing pain.

But in church, before the congregation, Pastor Nehemiah Gumbo and Mai Gumbo put up a united front, as the church founders. They had to be role models of a good marriage for dating young men and women.

But deep down there were cracks in their marriage. They had sought counselling from their mentor, Pastor Dimba, but things had not improved.

Pastor Nehemiah had a nagging guilty feeling. *Was he being unfair to his wife? Was he allowing the devil to tempt him into sin?* He decided to fight the temptation. He knelt down and prayed.

***

Back at her flat, Rose sat on her bed in the evening, sipping a cup of tea, and playing back the events of the day, in her mind. She took out the business card that Pastor Nehemiah had given her.

She remembered his darting chameleon eyes peering at her cleavage. *Why did he give her his business card? Should she call him? To say what?* She didn't want drama with another married lover, not after Rodney. She wouldn't phone Pastor Nehemiah.

She read the letter from Rodney. A sensation of fear tugged her senses. She dreaded his violent outbursts. She wished he could disappear from her life for good. What did he mean by 'getting even?' She checked her handbag for the pepper spray.

Then she thought about Brother Kudakwashe and his good singing voice, and felt goosebumps erupting on her skin. Blood whooshed through her veins. He would make a good boyfriend.

2

Rose arrived five minutes early for the 7pm Tuesday night choir practice at Paradise Life Pentecostal Ministries Church. She wore a figure-hugging tan dress. Her face was smeared with light brown make-up. The perfume was loud.

Her heart leaped with joy as she walked into the church auditorium and set eyes on Brother Kudakwashe. He was smartly dressed as usual in a shiny navy tuxedo and white trousers.

Gazes fastened on Rose as she walked over to Brother Kudakwashe. There were giggles and cryptic remarks that her dressing was inappropriate for the choir rehearsals. But Rose was unflustered by the remarks.

'Welcome to choir practice, Rose,' Brother Kudakwashe said, smiling and shaking her hand. He turned to the other choir members. 'Let's welcome Rose.' He made a gesture of open arms. 'She will be joining our choir practice.'

A coy smile formed on Rose's face as she acknowledged the choir members. They responded with friendly smiles and welcomed her with hugs and handshakes. Rose kept beaming.

But one choir member, a woman, neither smiled, nor hugged nor shook Rose's hand. She gave a thumbs up sign.

Rose was taken aback by her unfriendliness, but she feigned a smile at her.

During the rehearsals, Brother Kudakwashe beckoned Rose. 'Come forward and sing us your favourite hymn.'

Rose mustered her guts and came forward. She sang the hymn, *Amazing Grace*.

Most of the choir members clapped for Rose and nodded in approval after she finished singing. 'Your voice is good,' said awestruck Brother Kudakwashe.

Rose noticed that the odd woman neither clapped nor cheered. She just stared at her like she was a blank page in a book.

Rose blushed.

During the break, the odd woman approached Rose. 'I'm Maidei. Honestly, I think you must improve on your voice projection.'

'Thanks,' Rose forced a smile. 'Everyone seemed to like my singing though,' she said. Maidei strolled off.

'Ignore her,' said one choir member to Rose. She had overheard the conversation. 'Maidei is Brother Kudakwashe's ex-girlfriend. He ended the relationship because she was too possessive. But she still loves him. She is jealous of any woman who she thinks may attract Brother Kudakwashe's eye in the choir.'

'I see. What is your name?' Rose shook the woman's hand.

'Chengetai.'

Rose couldn't help it. She was attracted to Brother Kudakwashe's magnetic field, his aura and radiance. She would woo him with her good singing voice. *Tough luck, Maidei. The boy is mine. You're dealing with the wrong kind of girl. I am the attractive Rose.*

After choir practice, Maidei approached Rose again, 'Please stop gazing at Brother Kudakwashe with your lustful eyes.'

'I beg your pardon!' Rose glared at Maidei, 'What is your problem? How about you leave me alone?'

'You think I have not seen how you have been eyeing and salivating for Brother Kudakwashe like a dog yearning for a juicy bone?'

'What! You calling me a dog now? Do I look like a dog to you, bitch?' Rose raised her voice.

Everyone in the choir looked daggers at Rose.

'You obviously don't look like a dog,' Maidei said with a scornful gaze. 'I was metaphorically speaking that you've been salivating for Brother Kudakwashe like Pavlov's dog.'

'How dare you talk to Rose like that? I won't allow you to insult Rose that way, in front of everyone. You should apologise now!' Brother Kudakwashe stood between Rose and Maidei.

'Apologise? Didn't she just call me a bitch? Did she apologise for that? I won't apologise. I am only stating the obvious.'

'Watch your mouth, Maidei. I won't take another insult from you,' Rose was breathing heavily and fought the urge to pounce on her like a tigress.

'I will not allow such rude remarks in my choir. Both of you must apologise to each other now or else I will remove you both from my choir. Do you two hear me loud and clear?' Brother Kudakwashe menacing eyes glared at Maidei and Rose.

'I am sincerely sorry for my rude comments,' Maidei said, rolling her eyes.

'Sorry, I called you the inappropriate B word.' Rose glanced at Maidei from toe to head and extended her hand.

They shook their hands. But Rose was fizzing with anger in her mind.

A frosty relationship remained between Rose and Maidei in the choir during the next choir rehearsals. Maidei formed a clique that criticised everything that Rose did. With time, Rose increasingly felt picked on.

***

One Tuesday evening there was a disagreement among the choir members over who should lead the first Praise and Worship song at the Sunday service. Some choir members preferred Rose to lead, because she had the right tone of voice for the song, but others preferred Maidei instead. But Brother Kudakwashe said he would take time to pick the lead singer.

Rose felt snubbed by Brother Kudakwashe's indecisiveness. But she was determined to stay in the choir and win his affection.

After choir practice, Chengetai came over to Rose. 'Is the rumour true?'

'What rumour?'

'That you are a divorced single mum trying to honey trap Brother Kudakwashe.'

'What! Who is spreading those lies?'

'Maidei.'

Rose screwed her face like an angry lioness. She clenched her fists and charged towards Maidei. 'Why have you been spreading lies about me?'

'What lies?' Maidei muttered.

'That I'm a divorced single mum bent on seducing Brother Kudakwashe?'

'I never said that,' Maidei appeared shocked.

'You did, you lying bitch,' Rose delivered a hard punch to Maidei's face and knocked her down. 'That's for your lies, bitch.'

Rose spit into Maidei's face.

'Stop it, Rose! Stop it!' Brother Kudakwashe yanked Rose away from Maidei.

'This is unacceptable behaviour, inside the House of the Lord,' said Brother Kudakwashe, with his bemused eyes fastened on Rose. 'You must apologise to Maidei.'

Maidei got up clutching her bleeding nose.

'I won't apologise,' Rose walked away in a fit of uncontrollable rage.

'You are fired from the choir for unacceptable behaviour,' Brother Kudakwashe yelled after Rose.

Rose slammed the door hard on her way out.

Hours later, alone in her flat, Rose came to her senses and realised that she had behaved inappropriately in church, and she felt remorseful. She phoned Brother Kudakwashe to apologise. But he didn't answer the call.

***

Meanwhile, Mai Gumbo sat on the couch watching CNN evening news bulletin on tv. She lowered the volume and reminisced on the state of her marriage.

Twenty years before, she had married Pastor Nehemiah Gumbo, a God-fearing husband, and had been blessed with two lovely children, Tadiwanashe and Anesu, and co-foundered the thriving city church, Paradise Life Ministries Pentecostal

Church. But why did a dark cloud of despair hang over her life and marriage when she had a lot to be grateful for?

Her main concern was that Pastor Nehemiah now devoted most of his time to growing his church, thereby leaving little quality time with the family. He rarely touched her love handles nor complemented her for her gorgeous outfits and wigs. He often came to bed late and snored like a pig.

'Why are you spending too much time in church than with me and the children?' Mai Gumbo had asked him one night in the bedroom.

'I am very busy doing the Lord's work. I must expand my ministry,' he said, taking off his clothes and putting on a clean pair of pyjamas. 'You must support me instead of always sulking.'

'Are you implying that I no longer support your ministerial work? Didn't I stand by you when we founded this church and ministry? Aren't I a loyal and supportive wife? Now, you barely spend time home with me and the children, but you accuse me of not being supportive. You crawl into bed late and barely touch me. I didn't leave my parents' home for *Sadza* only. There is plenty of *Sadza* at their home. We must go for couples' counselling.'

'I am too busy for couples' counselling. I must improve the media production ministry and set up a new church website. The least you can do is support me.'

'I'm a supportive wife. It is you who has become the problem. You no longer listen to me. Pride has gone to your head. You are a senior pastor in the church, not in our house. Beware that pride comes before a fall.'

'I can't stand your whining. Menopause has unhinged the screws off your head. You have become a grumpy middle-aged woman.'

'What's my menopause got to do with our marriage? You are the one spending less time with your family. You must apologise for your rude menopause remarks.' Mai Gumbo had begun to cry.

'Sorry,' Pastor Nehemiah caressed her. She pushed him away at arm's length. 'Sorry, Darling. I will make time. We will go on holiday when I have finished the current project.'

'It has been over a year since we went on a family holiday.' Mai Gumbo scowled her face.

'We will go when I have finished setting up the media production ministry and the new church website is up and running. I promise you.'

They snuggled in bed and made passionate love.

3

The following day, Rose's mum had high blood pressure. 'I think you must be checked out by the doctors at Parirenyatwa hospital. I will take you there now,' Rose said.

Inside the hospital examination room, a young doctor said, 'I think you have other underlying medical issues than just high blood pressure. The lumps on your breast are concerning.' He gazed at Rose's mum and then at Rose. 'We will take bloods and run some tests to rule out breast cancer.'

'Breast cancer! That can't be it,' Rose shook her head. She glanced at the doctor, then at mum tilting her head.

'The test results must be ready tomorrow. Your mum will stay in hospital overnight and get checked on the blood pressure too.'

Rose hugged her mum. She had been the hen that shielded her from danger under her wings. It was heartbreaking to see her struggling with her health. She had always been a healthy and resilient mum.

Rose returned to her flat. That night Rose had a nightmare in which the doctor was telling her that mum was dead. She woke up with a start, sweating. She was relieved that it was only a bad dream.

***

The following day, Rose visited mum in hospital. 'Good morning, mum. Did you sleep well? Have you got the test results?'

'Sadly, the test results have confirmed that I have breast cancer. The doctor has recommended that I undergo chemotherapy.'

'Oh, no! Oh God!'

'Chemotherapy? And how much does it cost?'

'$20 000 USD'

'Gosh! And where do the doctors expect us to find such a huge sum of money for treatment? I don't have such money. I doubt if I will ever find someone to loan me this huge amount of money, in these hard times.'

'I have saved only $2000 USD. I would welcome any financial assistance from you, Rose. You can't just watch me die,' mum began to sob.

Rose hugged and caressed her on the back. She didn't want to lose her mum to cancer.

Mum looked up to the heavens, and muttered, 'Lord, I want to live to see my grandchildren.'

'You must worry about the treatment now, mum. Worry about the grandchildren when you have finished treatment and are in remission.'

'I don't want to die before you get married, and I cradle my grandchild in my arms.'

'Be patient, mum. You will be the first to know when I find the right man to marry me. I don't want to repeat the same mistake I made with Rodney.'

There was a momentary silence. Rose hugged her mum.

***

Rose looked through her handbag and found the business card that Pastor Nehemiah had given her on the first Sunday service. She needed someone to talk to about her mum's cancer diagnosis and the money woes.

Besides, she wanted to apologise to Pastor Nehemiah for the assault on Maidei. She hoped Pastor Nehemiah would tell Brother Kudakwashe that she had come for counselling on her anger management problems and hopefully, Brother Kudakwashe would forgive and readmit her to the choir.

Rose visited Pastor Nehemiah's office for counselling on a Tuesday afternoon.

Pastor Nehemiah looked intently at her figure-hugging mint dress and at her face. 'You look sad. It shows that your mum's cancer diagnosis has taken away your pretty smile. Shall we offer a prayer to the Lord, that by his stripes your mum will be healed?' He led a lengthy prayer.

There was momentary silence as Pastor Nehemiah cleared the papers on his desk.

'It's a double whammy; mum's cancer diagnosis and the exorbitant treatment fees. I don't want to see her die before I have raised the required treatment fees. I don't know how I will raise the money for the medical bill.'

'The church has a compassion ministry,' Pastor Nehemiah shifted in his chair. 'We will discuss the ways that the church can support you during this trying time. I can visit your mum in the hospital and pray for her.'

'My mum won't allow you to pray for her,' said Rose. 'She hates charismatic pastors of Pentecostal churches. She goes to a traditional church.'

There was a momentary silence. 'I hear you assaulted Maidei during choir practice. Why did you do such a shameful thing like that in the House of the Lord? Maidei wanted to report you to the police, and she changed her mind after counselling.'

'Maidei had been bitching about me since I joined the choir. She accused me of trying to seduce Brother Kudakwashe. I wasn't having any of that.' Rose had a stern look on her face.

'This is the House of the Lord, and you must demonstrate love and forgiveness when fellow believers offend you. We are different from the outside world where people settle scores with an eye for an eye. We forgive in church. Christianity is a way of life built on love and forgiveness.'

'I am sincerely sorry for overreacting. It won't happen again.' There was a remorseful look on Rose's face.

'I don't tolerate such unchristian behaviour inside my church. Why are you such an angry young woman? Tell me your story.'

Rose cleared her throat. 'I am an only child and raised by a single mum.'

'Where was your dad?'

'He abandoned us when I was seven. He has another family.'

'Are you still angry with him?'

'Of course. I would love to shoot him in the head if I had a gun, for abandoning my mum and me. Mum raised me on her own while my dad canoodled with a younger woman, in his small house.'

'You must be forgiving, Rose.'

'I can't do that.'

'You must forgive him, just as you have been forgiven by Christ.'

'Forgive? No way. I want to see the bastard burn in hell.'

'How did your mother manage financially, without your dad?'

'Well, mum is a tough woman. She worked hard as a vegetable vendor and still managed to send me to the University of Zimbabwe where I trained and qualified as an English Teacher.'

'What type of a parent was she?'

'Mum was strict and overprotective. At times she was very bossy. But she always had high expectations of me.'

'Every good parent wants the best for their child.'

'I know. But I don't want to feel pressured by her into getting married and having children. In case, I end up marrying the wrong man. I want to choose my future husband at my own time.'

'I see that you are an independent young woman. Nothing wrong with that. But the bible teaches us to respect our parents. What church does your mum attend?'

'She attends the Anglican Church. She thinks that the new Pentecostal churches are led by "the fake pastors and charlatans preaching the prosperity gospel and misleading people away from God."'

'She is entitled to her own opinions. You said something about your mum's medical bills. How much is required?'

'18 000 USD.'

'I would like to help her pay for the treatment bill from my own income. But promise me that you will not tell anyone when I have helped you financially. It must remain a secret.'

Rose was full of joy but kept calm.

Suddenly, Mai Gumbo burst into the office. 'Sorry I didn't know you were talking to someone,' she eyed Rose suspiciously.

'I was counselling and praying for Rose. Her mum has been diagnosed with breast cancer. Her mum will undergo chemotherapy. I have invited her to our home for lunch on Saturday and she has accepted.'

Rose remained quiet.

'You are welcome to visit us for lunch,' Mai Gumbo said, smiling at Rose.

'Thank you, Pastor Nehemiah. Thank you, Mai Gumbo. I must get going now.'

'You are welcome. Have a good day? Pass our greetings to your mum.' Pastor Nehemiah shifted in his chair. Rose stood up and left the office.

There was some silence. 'Since when have you started to invite people to our home without checking with me first?' There was anger on Mai Gumbo's face.

'Sorry, I was going to do so. Rose is going through a difficult time right now with her mum unwell. I thought this would be a good opportunity to offer counselling.'

'Alright. But just remember that I am the wife, the mother, and the gatekeeper of our home.'

'I know that.'

'When are we going on a family holiday? Everybody else is going on holiday except us. Even the almighty God rested on the seventh day. Why don't we go on a family vacation sooner?'

'I thought we already talked about that issue at home.'

'You are always making empty promises.'

'I will be all yours after I finish the current project. We will go on a family vacation to Cape Town soon.'

'I will only trust your word when I am on board the plane to Cape Town,' Mai Gumbo left the office.

4

Rose pondered whether to go for lunch with Pastor Nehemiah and his family that Saturday afternoon. She didn't want them to know too much about her life story. She didn't want to be read like a character in a book. But eventually, she decided to go anyway. She would keep certain secret pages of her life closed from them.

Mai Gumbo picked Rose from Westgate Shopping Mall. She had a snide look on her face. She drove her Volvo S40 through the tarred roads of the leafy suburb to her home. She was grumpy and barely spoke on the way.

Rose felt uncomfortable and wished she hadn't come.

Mai Gumbo stopped before an electric gate. The gate opened automatically, and she drove into a sprawling yard with a big house with a sky-blue colour and lush green lawns.

'Welcome to our home,' Mai Gumbo smiled. 'Would you like me to show you around the yard?'

'Yes, please.'

She showed Rose the flower beds with Roses, Periwinkles and Bougainvillea. There were vegetable gardens. A broad smile was planted on Mai Gumbo's face.

They went inside the house. 'Can I pour you a drink?'

'Yes, please,' said Rose.

Mai Gumbo showed Rose around the big house with expensive furniture.

'Where did you buy such beautiful, exotic furniture?'

'We imported it from Dubai.'

'This is very expensive furniture.'

'Pastor Nehemiah has close friends and business associates in Dubai. He imported the furniture at low duty. He has a lot of connections at the Customs Office.'

Rose longed to live in such a lap of luxury. *So, the money paid in, by congregants, as tithes and offerings, was funding such a lavish lifestyle? So, poor people lived in reeks of abject poverty, unemployment and disease and parted with their hard-earned cash after Pastor Nehemiah bamboozled them with his prosperity gospel?*

'So how long have you been married to Pastor Nehemiah?'

'Twenty years now. Every marriage has its challenges but thank God that we are still together. Do you have a boyfriend, Rose?'

'No.'

'Why not?' Mai Gumbo was curious. 'You are such a beautiful young woman who must settle down to a married life soon.' Rose averted her eyes.

'Do you want me to be the match maker? You know, match you to an eligible bachelor in the church?'

Rose screwed her face. 'No thank you.' *This woman who barely knew her was taking pity on her and offering to match her to an eligible bachelor in the church. How condescending. Nice try. But no, thank you.*

At lunch Pastor Nehemiah kept stealing glances at Rose. She felt uncomfortable like the first day in church during the Sunday service. He kept kicking her under the table. She asked how they had started the church and the challenges that they had faced.

Pastor Nehemiah said he had felt disgruntled as a pastor in a former big church. And he had felt a strong calling by God to form his own church. He had been obedient and started from humble beginnings.

After lunch, Pastor Nehemiah offered to drive Rose into town. During the drive he started to flirt with Rose. She cringed when he kept touching her on the knees. 'Please stop that.'

He laughed. He gave her a gold necklace that he had bought in Dubai.

'No, I can't take that. Why are you giving it to me?'

'Because I am attracted to you, and I can't help it. So, I am gifting you this necklace. Please accept it.'

Eventually Rose accepted the gold necklace and thanked him. It was beautiful. She had a passion for nice stuff like jewellery, expensive perfumes, cool outfits, and handbags. But she couldn't afford these on her low teacher's salary.

After Pastor Nehemiah dropped Rose off at the commuter omnibus station, he was happy she had accepted the necklace. He decided to lavish her with more expensive gifts until he stole her heart.

He knew Rose's Achilles heel; the pent-up anger she had towards her dad for deserting her and her mother and her desperation for funds to pay her mother's medical bill. Rose needed cheering up, *poor thing*. He would play his cards right and be her shoulder to cry on. He hoped this would blossom into a titillating affair.

***

Meanwhile, Rose went to see her mother at Parirenyatwa Hospital. She asked mum how she had been. Mum looked sullen and spoke slowly. She was visibly in pain. She said the doctors were insisting on her starting treatment as soon as possible. But she had to pay the money first.

Rose felt sympathy for her and reassured her that she would find the funds soon.

'Where will you get the money?'

'Well, desperate times require desperate measures, mum.'

'And what does that mean? Don't go and rob a bank.'

Rose laughed. 'No, mum, I'm not going to hold up a bank. Don't worry mum. I will borrow the money from church friends.'

'Don't do anything illegal to get the money. Please, don't.'

'I won't.'

On the way home, Rose took a commuter omnibus into the city centre. She was depressed and strolled along First Street doing some window shopping. There were some pretty outfits displayed in the window at the Edgars shop.

Then, she heard a familiar sounding voice. She turned around and saw Brother Kudakwashe strolling leisurely with Maidei. They were holding hands and giggling like teenagers in love.

Rose hid behind a pillar. Brother Kudakwashe planted a kiss on Maidei's cheek. She smooched him on the mouth.

Rose felt faint and staggered away in a daze. She was heartbroken. So, Maidei had won Brother Kudakwashe's heart, in the end? She wished she was the one strolling in the city with Brother Kudakwashe at dusk. She felt an urge to return and wrestle Brother Kudakwashe from Maidei. But she walked away.

Rose was distraught on the way to her flat. Her mum had breast cancer, and she had lost the fight to win the heart of Brother Kudakwashe. Now saving her mum was her priority.

She thought about Pastor Nehemiah. *Was he the panacea to her problems?* She needed to catch him hook, line, and sinker. That was the only viable option to save her mum.

A girl had to do what a girl had to do, when faced with a mum with breast cancer and exorbitant hospital bills. She would play along with Pastor Nehemiah's game.

She remembered her past blesser, Rodney, the businessman, back in the university days. It had been a win-win situation. She provided him with the sexual gratification that he craved for, and he funded her comfortable lifestyle on university campus. Now she saw Pastor Nehemiah as a means to an end, her meal ticket.

She remembered how things had got complicated with Rodney. He had become more abusive, controlling and possessive, and she wanted out of the relationship. She had hatched a disingenuous escape plan and got a few thousand US dollars off him. She made the sucker pay.

5

'Can you please come to my office after the service?' Pastor Nehemiah winked at Rose at the church door on Tuesday night.

'Alright,' Rose smiled and sashayed into the church in a black miniskirt and white top showing cleavage that attracted stares from the congregants. Her seductive attire and smooth face with a layer of brown foundation attracted leery eyes of men in church.

Pastor Nehemiah preached about the parable of the Good Samaritan and beseeched the congregants to help out fellow human beings who are in trouble. He preached with clarity and conviction.

After the service, Rose knocked on the heavy, teak door and entered Pastor Nehemiah's spacious and well-ventilated office. He sat on a comfortable, black leather swivelling chair behind a shiny, mahogany desk. A fragrance of lavender wafted in the air.

'Thanks for coming, Rose. Please sit down.' He rolled his big eyes and gazed at her from head to toe. 'You look immaculate.'

'Thanks.' Rose avoided his piercing eyes and sat on the empty chair. She swivelled in the chair.

'I'll provide you with the full payment of your mother's medical treatment bill.'

Rose's jaw dropped. 'Thank you.'

'I know you love your mum very much. That is the least I can do to help.'

'Thank you. How long will it take to repay the loan?'

'Well, you won't need to repay the money, if you repay me in kind. You and I can get closely acquainted.'

'Closely acquainted?'

'Yes.'

'What do you mean?'

'You're obviously a gorgeous, young woman. And I am obviously attracted to you; by your sense of humour, grooming and style. You and I could get something special going between us.'

Rose was mute and gazed at him.

'Well, I want us to know each other at a deeper intimate level.'

'So, in other words, you want me to be your girlfriend?' Rose put on a seductive lost kitten look. 'What if your wife discovered us having an affair?'

'How is she going to find out? Do you intend to tell her?'

'No.'

'Even if you told her. I would deny it and accuse you of telling lies.'

'How do you live with yourself? You have just been on the platform preaching about righteousness, and then the next moment, you are hitting on me?'

'All of us are sinners, Rose. We are always showing a beautiful façade of ourselves to the outside world but underneath there is a volcano of sin waiting to spew out like lava.'

'Where is your bible trained conscience?'

'I have it. But that doesn't make me a saint. I am only human, and I covet a gorgeous woman like you.'

'Why are you preaching a lie in front of the congregation?'

'I preach what they want to hear, what titillates their minds. "The gospel is opium of the mind, said Karl Marx."'

'Don't you think you are living a lie that runs parallel to what you preach? Such a high level of hypocrisy must displease God,' Rose said as she stood up.

'Oh, come on now, Rose. Please sit down.'

'I am caught between a rock and a hard place,' muttered Rose.

'I can't help it. I'm so attracted to you, Rose. Please give me your heart.'

'I don't know.' Rose looked at the mountain of hundreds of US dollar bills and then at Pastor Nehemiah.

She blushed. She was confused and flattered. His words made her feel mature and womanly.

'Please accept the money.' He showed her the new, shiny crisp banknotes.

Rose's eyes rolled.

'Okay, let me help you pack the money.' He shoved the bills into a satchel. 'A rose by any means is pretty. Here you are,' he handed the satchel to Rose.

Rose hesitated and then accepted the satchel. 'Thank you.' She left the office.

Mai Gumbo saw Rose leaving the office with the satchel. She began to suspect that there was something going on between Pastor Nehemiah and Rose.

First, she had walked into his office and found Rose there. Then he had invited her to their home for lunch and now she was coming out of his office again. She wondered what was in the satchel.

Mai Gumbo was overwhelmed with jealousy. *What if Pastor Nehemiah was having an affair with her? How could he cheat on her with a younger woman after twenty years of marriage?* Maybe he was just praying for her sick mother. She decided to keep an eye on her.

***

Rose pondered whether she had done the right thing, accepting the money from Pastor Nehemiah. Yes, she needed the money to pay for her mum's chemotherapy treatment. *But what would he want in return? Would she be able to provide him all that he craved for? Poor Pastor Nehemiah, a middle-aged pastor who stood on the pulpit putting up a façade of piety but was starved of affection at home.*

But could his money buy the love that he craved for? She would give him the affection he craved for, in return for her mum's treatment. It was a win-win situation.

But had she also lost her conscience? In tough times a girl had to do what she had to do, to bait the goldfish. *But what would be the consequences of these shenanigans?*

6

The following day, Rose went to the Parirenyatwa hospital and paid off her mum's medical bill.

'Where did you get the money, Rose?' mum repositioned herself on the hospital bed.

'I borrowed the money from a church friend. I will repay her the loan with interest.'

'God bless your generous friend. It is difficult to find such a generous friend in Harare in these hard times. Your friend was heaven sent.'

'Yes, mum,' Rose smiled. She drew closer to her mother and stroked her unkempt hair. Then she patted her on the shoulder and head. 'Best wishes with the chemotherapy. See you tomorrow, mum.' Tears glistened in Rose's eyes.

As Rose walked through the corridors of the hospital, she wondered how mum would react the day she learned that the money for the medical bill had actually come from Pastor Nehemiah, and she had agreed to have an affair with him. Mum would probably have a heart attack. *Poor mum, she had such high hopes for her, but she was living a lie before her eyes.*

***

Pastor Nehemiah visited Rose's flat that evening. He knocked hard on the door. Rose peeped through the spy hole and her heart pulsated when she saw him. She had not invited him to her flat, but there he was, standing outside the door, smiling, and holding a bouquet of flowers and some groceries.

She hesitated, and slowly opened the door. 'Welcome to my humble flat, Man of God,' Rose smiled.

'Hello, my beautiful Rose,' Pastor Nehemiah smiled like a smitten teenager. He hugged and kissed her. He handed her the golden daffodils and groceries. He strolled casually into the lounge.

'Beautiful flowers. Thank you for the groceries. Would you like a cup of tea or coffee, Man of God?' Rose rolled her bashful eyes.

'Gin and tonic on the rocks will do. Just kidding. Yes, a cup of tea will do. Thanks.'

Rose went to the kitchen and made tea in a big mug. She made herself diluted *Mazoe* squash in a glass.

Pastor Nehemiah sat next to her on the sofa and caressed her on the shoulder. She tensed her body and avoided eye contact.

'How is your mum?'

'She started chemo this afternoon.'

'Good. Did she ask where you got the money?'

'Yes, she did.'

'And what did you say?'

'I told her that a female church friend had loaned me the money. I dare not tell her it was you. Mum would put two and two together and figure out what was really going on between us.'

He laughed. 'Now you see. Everyone tells lies, even you, my beautiful Rose. Though, others tell bigger lies than others.'

Rose was bashful.

He suddenly planted a kiss on Rose's cheek.

'Not so fast. Take it easy, Man of God. It takes time to woo the heart of a woman.'

'What do you mean?'

'Well, you must be sensitive to the mood of the woman.'

'Where did you learn all that romantic stuff?'

'Mills and Boon novels.'

'Holy crap. Did you have any affairs in the past?'

'No, I didn't. I was a good girl until you made me a bad girl.'

'Good. I can't stand and watch another man take you away, my beautiful Rose.'

They stared at each other and laughed.

'Anyway, it has been good to see you, my beautiful Rose.' He downed his cup of tea. 'I must get going. I've an important meeting at the church. I love you.' Pastor Nehemiah smooched Rose on the mouth.

Rose rolled her eyes like a teenager smooched for the first time.

He took out his wallet from his hip pocket. 'Here is some money. Buy yourself a pretty dinner dress. I will take you out to a posh, private restaurant at the Rainbow Towers.'

'That would be nice.' Rose saw him to the door. He kissed her again on the cheek. She waved at him shyly and shut the door behind her.

She counted the crisp twenty US dollar notes. They were five hundred US dollars. *He is a generous man, she thought. Bless him for knowing that I need a pretty dinner dress.* She expected more money from him for other goodies like expensive perfumes, nice outfits, cool shoes, and matching handbags.

She no longer minded the shenanigans with him. Well, they were two consenting adults, engaged in a consensual affair, she reasoned.

Life is a game of poker; you win or lose. But the game of poker must end. *Would it end in joy or tears?* They were both putting on a façade to an illicit affair that would one day run its course. She would play the game while she could.

***

The following day, Rose received a bouquet of flowers at her workplace on her 26th birthday.

'These are beautiful flowers,' said Gamuchirai, Rose's work mate, stroking the golden daffodils and red roses. 'Do you have a new boyfriend, Rose? How come you didn't fill me in?'

'I don't know who sent them. It must be a secret admirer from church.'

'This person really has an eye for you. The flowers are so lovely. I wish I had someone to show me such love, on my birthday, with these beautiful flowers.'

'Be patient, you will soon find a man who looks like Mane, the footballer.'

'Oh yes, Mane will do it, any time of the day. Lucky you, Rose.'

Rose was baffled. *Who had sent the flowers? Why did the sender remain anonymous?* Maybe Pastor Nehemiah didn't want to give away his true identity.

***

Later that afternoon, Rose received a text message from Brother Kudakwashe asking if she had received the flowers that he had sent her. Rose was shocked. He asked her to call him and arrange a birthday lunch date. But she didn't.

Then Brother Kudakwashe called her.

'What can I do for you?' Rose asked.

'Can we go out on a lunch date, please?'

'No. I don't have the time.'

'Please give me one opportunity to spoil you.'

'I said, no.'

'We must talk.'

'Talk about what?'

'You and I dating and becoming soul mates.'

Rose laughed. 'That won't happen. Maidei is your type, not me. Nice try. Bye, good luck.' Rose ended the phone call. She dumped all the flowers in the bin.

***

That evening, Pastor Nehemiah took Rose out for dinner at the swanky Harvest Garden Restaurant with a view of the pool and gardens at the Rainbow Towers Hotel. It was an ideal hideout. Low music played in the background.

Rose ordered a plate of rice served with spicy chicken and coleslaw salad. Pastor Nehemiah ordered *Sadza* with a platter of *Boerwoers* sausages, flame grilled chicken and a leafy salad on the side.

At the start of the night, Rose was quiet and guarded, but as the night progressed, she drank a glass of wine. She lost her inhibitions and became talkative. Their conversations were on church politics, prosperity gospel, Pastor Nehemiah's marital issues, and their affair.

Afterwards, Pastor Nehemiah drove to her flat and carried her across the threshold of the door. He French-kissed her. Rose wilted in his arms. She hugged and kissed him. Then he carried her to the bedroom in his strong arms and undressed her on the king-size bed. They wrestled on the bed in a matchup of wild passion and desire.

'I love you,' he said afterwards, putting on his clothes and kissing her. 'I will see you tomorrow, my beautiful Rose.'

'I love you too.'

Pastor Nehemiah left.

Rose had given herself to him. He was a real hard *MaShona* stud in bed. She was also confused. *Was she cheap to hop into bed on a first date? Did she let her guard down too soon?* The wine seemed to have distracted her from understanding what she was doing.

She wondered if she had consented to the love making or one thing had led to the other. *Where was this affair heading?* She took a contraceptive pill.

That night, Rose missed the warmth of Pastor Nehemiah's strong arms. She texted love emojis to him.

He texted back heart emojis.

She smiled and fell asleep.

7

On Friday night, Pastor Nehemiah took Rose to another restaurant, Kombahari restaurant, also at Rainbow Towers Hotel. It was cosy inside the restaurant. Low, romantic music played in the background. Couples canoodled inside the dimly lit restaurant.

Rose was talking about her mum's chemotherapy treatment when she heard a familiar voice behind her. She turned and saw Brother Kudakwashe and two men walk past and sit on an opposite table.

Rose avoided eye contact with Brother Kudakwashe. Her heart pummelled.

'Why have you stopped talking?' Pastor Nehemiah gazed at her.

Her laser eyes punned on Brother Kudakwashe and his friends. Their eyes met. Rose looked down at her dinner plate.

Brother Kudakwashe was shocked to see Rose with Pastor Nehemiah inside the restaurant. He waved at her, and she barely acknowledged him.

'What's the matter, my beautiful Rose? Are you alright?' Pastor Nehemiah noticed Rose's uneasiness.

'Nothing.'

'You stopped talking when Brother Kudakwashe walked in with his friends.'

'I am worried about what he will say in church about seeing you and me, here.'

'Don't worry. I will manage this.' Pastor Nehemiah nodded at Brother Kudakwashe. He got up and walked over to him. He greeted and patted him on the shoulder. He cracked a joke and they burst out laughing.

Moments later Pastor Nehemiah returned to the table.

'What did you say to him?' Rose asked.

'I told him that I had gone to pray for your sick mother at Parirenyatwa Hospital and decided to take you out for a counselling session over dinner. He believed me. Now eat your food like my good girl.'

Rose couldn't tell Pastor Nehemiah about the bouquet of flowers that Brother Kudakwashe had sent her today, and that he had asked her out on a date. And that she had turned him down. And here he was glaring at her like a hungry dog eyeing a rabbit.

Rose ate slowly, and almost choked on the chips and flame grilled beef steaks.

Brother Kudakwashe had discovered their cosy hideout. What would he do next? Would he tell Mai Gumbo and the whole church what he had seen? How would Mai Gumbo react? How would she wriggle out of this tight corner?

Brother Kudakwashe continued stealing glances at Rose. But she looked away.

Rose talked less. The joy of the dinner date had turned to uneasiness.

Eventually, Brother Kudakwashe and his friends left the restaurant.

Rose sighed.

'Don't worry about him. I am the Senior Pastor of Paradise Life Ministries. I will defend our meeting if the grapevine spreads. It's Brother Kudakwashe's word against mine,' said Pastor Nehemiah grinning, as he drove her home. He kissed her goodbye at the flat door and went away.

***

Rose pondered whether to attend Sunday service. *What if the whole church already knew about her secret affair with Pastor Nehemiah? What if Mai Gumbo confronted her about it? How would she react? Would she confirm or deny the affair?* She decided to go to church anyway.

Rose sat quietly inside the church auditorium, stealing glances at Mai Gumbo. She didn't glance back at her. She listened intently to Pastor Nehemiah Gumbo's sermon. He was preaching from the first book of Peter about husbands respecting their wives and wives respecting their husbands as heads of households.

Poor Mai Gumbo, soaking in the sermon about respect between husbands and wives. Unbeknown to you, he is having a bit by the side with me, Rose thought.

Brother Kudakwashe kept casting glances at Rose. She looked away.

Why was Pastor Nehemiah preaching lies in front of the congregation? This was hypocrisy. Why did he speak ill of his wife when they were together at their cosy rendezvous? Why was Mai Gumbo faithful to a man who was cheating on her? It was mind boggling how the supposed Man of God sinned behind the façade.

Brother Kudakwashe came to Rose after the service. 'What were you doing with Pastor Nehemiah at that restaurant?'

'He asked me out for dinner after praying for my mum in hospital. What's that got to do with you? You're neither my father nor my brother.'

'Having an affair with a married man is a sin before God, Rose.'

'Who told you I am having an affair with him?'

'I know that. I saw by the way you two cosied up to each other inside that restaurant.'

'You are free to draw your own conclusions. But the fact is that there is nothing going on between us,' Rose said nonchalantly.

'Nevertheless, beware of him. He has covetous eyes for gorgeous, single women like you. And going out on a dinner date with him sends the wrong signals.'

'What are you talking about? What wrong signals?' Rose appeared shocked.

'It may imply that you are having an affair with him.'

'Imply to whom?'

'To me or to members of the congregation.'

'Don't spread grapevine in the church. There is nothing going on between me and him.'

'I didn't say I would spread grapevine.'

'No need to worry yourself to death about things that are not happening nor don't concern you. He is old enough to be my dad, for heaven's sake.' Rose said with a straight face.

'Sorry, if I have upset you.'

'You have. Don't you dare go around the church spreading lies about an affair that doesn't exist.' Rose was pointing at him with her finger.

'Sorry, Rose. Can I at least take you out for lunch to clear the air?'

'Clear the air? What air?'

'We must go out on a date and be friends again.'

Rose laughed. 'That's a strange way of asking me out on a date. Firstly, you accuse me of having an affair with the Man of God, and then you ask me out on a date.'

'Sorry, Rose.'

'What happened between you and Maidei?'

'We broke up.'

'I saw you two doves strolling in the CBD the other night.'

'There was nothing going on between us.'

'Yeah, right. I don't trust you.'

'One day you will trust me,' Brother Kudakwashe said.

'And when will that be?'

'I am not giving up until you have fallen head over heels with me.'

'Good luck,' Rose sneered at him and strolled away. She was relieved that the grapevine had not spread around the church.

Brother Kudakwashe stared at Rose as she cat walked out of church. He enjoyed the thrill of pursuing a woman who played hard to get, and eventually winning the battle of wits. He was determined to date her.

***

In the sweltering afternoon, Rose sat alone and watched YouTube videos when the phone rang. She saw the caller ID and smiled.

133

'Can I come over for a chat, my beautiful Rose? I'm having a bad afternoon and could do with joyful company. Are you at home?' Pastor Nehemiah yawned.

'Yes, of course. Come over.'

Pastor Nehemiah rang the doorbell on her flat twenty minutes later. He had a plastic bag of groceries and a bouquet of flowers. He kissed Rose and sat next to her on the double sofa in the lounge.

'What's bugging you, Man of God?'

'The fake news on YouTube.'

'What fake news? There is a lot of fake news on social media these days.'

'Haven't you seen the fake news story about people going to Ximex Mall and getting their toes cut for money ritual purposes? That story is obviously fake news, but it has gone viral around the world.'

'What does the story of foreign currency dealers at Ximex Mall have to do with you?'

'Well, everything. The fake news has slowed down business. I have my boys buying and selling US dollars there, at Ximex Mall, on the black market.'

'No way! Why are you involved in buying and selling currency on the black market?'

'Because it is profitable business. I lend the profits from the black-market trading to gold buyers, the Gold Mafia. Then they repay the loan into my Dubai bank account. It is called the Wahala money transfer.'

'What other hidden things do you do, behind the beautiful façade, Man of God?'

'Nothing else. I want you as my second wife.'

'No. That's a no, no. Yes, we can have a bit by the side. But marrying you, that's a step too far. You are already married. I don't want to be a homewrecker. I would rather remain your small house.'

'I hear you, loud and clear, my beautiful Rose.' He kissed her.

8

Rose was having second thoughts about her affair with Pastor Nehemiah. *Had she gone too far with her shenanigans with Pastor Nehemiah? Where was the affair heading? What if Mai Gumbo discovered the affair? Should she call time on the affair?*

She had had her fun, but she didn't want to be named, shamed, and excommunicated from the church. Besides, she had got what she wanted from the affair, money to pay for mum's medical bill.

Rose had a recurring nightmare, in which she was caught red-handed by Mai Gumbo snuggled in bed with Pastor Nehemiah. She dreaded the dream becoming a reality. She had told Pastor Nehemiah about the dream. He had dismissed it as a mere bad dream.

'No, we can't end this special relationship,' said shocked Pastor Nehemiah.

'Yes, we should.'

'How can you repay me with such ingratitude? Not after all that I have done for you.' Pastor Nehemiah shook his head.

'Haven't I done something for you, too? Haven't I offered you my body and tender love and care that you craved for? Haven't I opened my inviting thighs to you? Haven't I brought you fun during your midlife crisis?'

'You have a strange way of demonstrating gratitude, my beautiful Rose.'

'Of course, I am grateful for the financial help you provided me when my mum had a huge hospital bill to pay. I gave you my listening ear. You were always whining about your nagging wife. But all good things must come to an end. This secret affair is morally wrong because you are a married pastor, and preacher of the true word of God. You and I are living a lie.'

'I can't help it, my beautiful Rose. I have goosebumps every time I set my eyes on you. There is nothing wrong with two consenting adults engaging in an affair. I love you too much to just let you go.'

'I wish you would stop preaching and living a lie, for God's sake. It is a sin. My conscience is troubled daily by this affair. In the end, I may have to leave the church.'

'Leave the church? Over what? Over the affair? You can't leave the church over that. No, I won't let you end something special between us.'

'Yes, I can.'

He exhaled and looked at her. 'Sorry, I was losing my temper with you. We have no option but to continue this relationship.'

'I don't want to.'

'I can't live without you.'

'How have you lived all these years without me?' Rose asked.

'I have been living a lie. But you made me find a new meaning to life. I had built a beautiful façade in front of my congregation, as a happily married man, but deep inside I was in turmoil. You came and made me clearly see the meaning of true love. We must continue seeing each other.'

'I don't know. My heart wants out.'

'You must reconsider your decision. We must go to Cape Town together on Friday.'

'I don't think so.'

'We'll go on Friday afternoon and return on Saturday evening. We can at least have our final tango in Cape Town. I will buy two return tickets to Cape Town.'

'I really don't want to go anywhere with you. I want to end this affair.'

Pastor Nehemiah whipped out a brown envelope, extracted crisp banknotes, and gave them to Rose. 'Buy a nice outfit and a bikini. There is a sandy beach in Cape Town.'

Rose handed back the banknotes. He left the banknotes on the coffee table. 'I know you will change your mind,' he winked and left the flat.

Rose looked at the banknotes. She counted them. $1000 USDs. She didn't know what to do with the money. She felt coerced into going to Cape Town.

Mum called minutes later. She was in a lot of pain. She sounded anxious over the phone.

The doctor had prescribed new, stronger pain relief medication.

Rose promised to buy her the prescription.

After mum's call, Rose pondered about going to Cape Town. Maybe he was right. She needed one last tango with him in Cape Town.

***

When Pastor Nehemiah arrived home, Mai Gumbo was waiting in the lounge. 'Where have you been? I have been phoning you. Today is our 21st wedding anniversary. Have you booked a table at our favourite restaurant?'

'No.'

'Why not?'

'I forgot.'

'Really, forgot? Yeah, right. You forgot that we have been married for twenty-one years today? How could you forget our wedding anniversary? Where have you been?'

'I was in a meeting with a Nigerian businessman who wanted US dollars to buy gold.'

'The least you could have done was answer my phone call. What is more important than telling your wife that you love her, on your wedding anniversary? What have you been really up to, Senior Pastor Nehemiah Gumbo?'

'I was really busy. Sorry I forgot about our wedding anniversary. We will go on a romantic date on Sunday night. Now, stop nagging me.'

'What! You're too busy to spend time with your wife on your wedding anniversary? You have been acting strange these days; you dress smart and go out every night and don't say where you are going, and you don't answer my calls. What is going on? Why are you as elusive as a mouse? What are you hiding? Lord knows what is going on. God forbid, you are not cheating on me. I will hit the roof of the sky.'

'I am not cheating on you.'

'If you do, I will cut off your manhood.'

'I wish you could trust me more, after all these years of married life. Instead, you are constantly nagging me due to your insecurities.'

'Trust you? When you forget our wedding anniversary. Trust you, when you're playing hide and seek with me. Trust you, when you ignore my phone calls. Trust you, when you're not spending quality time with me and children. Trust you? Lord, Jesus Christ, give me the grace to trust you.'

'Alright, I will make it up to you. We will wine and dine at one of the restaurants at Rainbow Towers Hotel restaurant on Sunday. But tomorrow, Friday, I must go to Cape Town on a business trip. I will buy you a special wedding anniversary gift there. I will return on Saturday evening.'

He went to take a bath. Mai Gumbo smelled his clothes. The clothes reeked of an aroma of Red door perfume. She shook her head. *So, this was what he was up to, cheating?*

She grabbed his tablet and attempted to log in. But the password had changed. 'Shit,' she muttered with disgust. She didn't want to start another big argument. She covered her head with the duvet cover and rolled towards the far end of the bed. She wept silently.

When Pastor Nehemiah returned from the bathroom, he was relieved to find his wife fast asleep. He checked his phone. Then he went into the empty, spare bedroom to make a call.

Meanwhile, Mai Gumbo got out of bed and tiptoed to the door. She could hear him raise his voice over the phone. 'You must come along with me. I have already bought two flight tickets. You must come along. I will show you around the beautiful city of Cape Town, do some shopping and walk along the sandy beach.'

She heard him end the call and she dashed back into bed. She slipped her head under the duvet cover and pretended to sleep. Tears welled in her eyes.

Pastor Nehemiah sat on the bed and fiddled with his phone. He went to the kitchen, leaving his phone. Mai Gumbo got up and peeked at the phone and jotted down the last number he called. She went back to sleep.

***

The following morning, Mai Gumbo struggled to contain the anger that was seething inside her. She made breakfast for Pastor Nehemiah and offered to drive him to Robert Mugabe International Airport. But he declined and booked a cab instead.

Mai Gumbo feigned a smile and wished him a safe journey. Soon after he left, she called a taxi to the airport. Anger was pounding through her chest. This was an opportunity to catch him red-handed with the woman that he was seeing.

There was traffic congestion along the airport road. Mai Gumbo begged the taxi driver to manoeuvre around the congestion because she wanted to see off someone at the airport before their flight. The driver begged her to be patient. The congestion finally eased, and the taxi driver accelerated on the straight, smooth highway to the airport.

Mai Gumbo ordered the taxi driver to wait while she went inside the airport departure hall. From a distance Mai Gumbo caught a glimpse of Pastor Nehemiah and Rose strolling arm in arm through the departure gate. It was too late to either take a photograph or yell at them. They disappeared into the departure lounge.

For a moment Mai Gumbo wanted to run and burst through the departure gate. But she knew that the airport security staff would not allow her through. Tears flowed down her cheeks as she returned to the waiting taxi.

Part Two

1

Rose and Pastor Nehemiah canoodled on the seats inside the packed departure lounge.

'You look immaculate in that navy blue dress,' Pastor Nehemiah's salivating tongue lolled out. His big hawk eyes coveted her from skull to sole.

'Thank you,' Rose smiled, exposing her pearly white teeth.

'Thanks for coming along with me to Cape Town. I appreciate that.' He gently stroked her face.

'You are welcome,' Rose rolled her eyes.

'Just wanted us to have some fun, in another country, far from prying eyes.'

'Though I am so excited about the getaway, I am also scared too; this is the first time I have been on board a plane.'

'There is always a first time to everything. Did your mum ask where you were going?' Pastor Nehemiah looked direct in her eyes.

'Yes. I told her that I was going to Mutare for a school trip. She was very happy for me.'

'I hope she does not phone the school and find out that you are not on a school trip but in Cape Town.'

'I don't think she will contact the school.'

'What did you tell your wife?'

'I told her that I was going on a business trip to Cape Town. She trusts me all the time.' Pastor Nehemiah fumbled through his hand luggage. Suddenly he put his hand over his mouth.

'What's the matter?'

'I forgot my iPad. I ordered the plane tickets on it. I hope my wife doesn't log on and read my emails and see the bank transactions.'

There was an announcement that passengers to Cape Town must start boarding the plane. Rose felt uneasiness in her belly. And her knees trembled.

She sat by the window and had a good outside view. She felt sick and asked an air hostess for a sick bag. Her intestines tightened as the plane taxied towards the runway. She vomited into the sick bag as the plane sped on the runway, took off and then rose higher into the pregnant clouds. Rose was scared that the plane might crash. So, she was awake on the whole flight.

***

Meanwhile, Mai Gumbo sat by the bedside, deep in thought when she saw the iPad under the pillow on the right side of the bed. She picked it up and tried a password that she knew.

Immediately, she logged on and read the emails. Her big eyes almost popped out with shock and rage when she saw the names on the two plane tickets and the times of the return flights.

She would confront Pastor Nehemiah with this evidence and demand answers. She felt betrayed and angry that Pastor Nehemiah had cheated on her.

And to rub salt on her wounds, he had taken that whore, Rose, to Cape Town instead of his family. He had not kept his promise. Mai Gumbo hated Rose like the devil. She had welcomed her into her house, but she had repaid her by stealing her husband. She tore her T-shirt in a fit of rage.

***

Rose was captivated by the panoramic view of the Drakensberg Mountains from the plane. And as the plane descended, she was awestruck by the beauty of Cape Town, sandwiched between Table Mountain and the Atlantic Ocean.

Pastor Nehemiah and Rose quickly checked out and collected their bags. They hired a taxi to the Commodore Hotel, situated adjacent to the V&A Waterfront, a 10-minute walk from Cape Town Stadium. The hotel had a 24-hour room service and 24-hour reception.

The bedrooms were spotless, spacious, tranquil with air-conditioning, free Wi-Fi, and satellite TV. There was a clean bathroom with a bathtub. Rose and Pastor Nehemiah bubble bathed in the tub.

Rose used the hair dryer, and she donned a white floral night dress.

'You look immaculate,' Pastor Nehemiah said, drooling over her.

Rose went outside on the balcony and gazed at the bright city lights and cars. The ocean waves glistened in the night from the distance.

Pastor Nehemiah and Rose changed into smart dinner clothes and went downstairs for a romantic dinner in the Clipper Restaurant which served an à la carte menu with delicious seafood dishes and regional wines.

After dinner they returned to the hotel bedroom. Pastor Nehemiah carried Rose over the threshold of the door and laid her on the bed. He unbuttoned her dress. He caressed her face, nipples and saddled on her. He massaged the gorges of her thighs and slowly eased into her.

He peered into her eyes as he thrusted and guided her into a frenzy of ecstasy. Rose moaned as he titillated her. After the marathon, he rolled off her, panting like a satisfied bull.

Afterwards, Rose watched a romantic film on one of the satellite channels on the Plasma tv. Pastor Nehemiah snored like a swine at the end of the bed.

***

The following morning, Mai Gumbo walked into Barclays bank in Harare city centre. She asked a teller for a bank statement of the joint account with Pastor Nehemiah. The bank teller handed her a printed statement.

When Mai Gumbo saw the remaining balance in the bank account, she bolted out of the bank in floods of tears. The bank teller was left shaking her head. A huge sum had been withdrawn from the account in one month.

Mai Gumbo phoned Pastor Nehemiah. But he didn't answer his phone. She was seething with rage.

2

The following morning, Pastor Nehemiah woke Rose up early. They made love again and bathed together in the bathtub. They dressed up in casual wear and went downstairs to the restaurant for breakfast. Amapiano music played low in the background. They both ordered a full English breakfast.

After breakfast, they returned to their hotel room. Rose watched tv in the hotel room while Pastor Nehemiah returned downstairs to the restaurant alone for a business meeting with a South African business partner.

He returned an hour later, grinning and showing off wads of South African rands. They went shopping in the central business district of Cape Town. Rose bought a gorgeous outfit, handbag, and expensive perfume.

Pastor Nehemiah bought an expensive outfit for his wife. He said it was a wedding anniversary gift. Rose felt jealous.

***

Mai Gumbo looked through the church records and found the phone number of Rose's next of kin, her mum. She phoned the number.

Rose's mum answered the phone call.

Mai Gumbo introduced herself and said that she had evidence that her daughter, Rose, was having an affair with her husband, Pastor Nehemiah. She wanted her to tell Rose to stop the affair with her husband.

Rose's mum said Mai Gumbo must have phoned the wrong number, because, as far as she knew, Rose was not seeing anyone at the moment. She had gone on a school trip.

Mai Gumbo laughed and told her that Rose was not on a school trip, but she was knocking boots with her husband in Cape Town at that time.

Rose's mum said she would confront Rose about the issue when she returned. She said she would be disappointed if this was true. She didn't want to talk much because she was in a lot of pain in hospital.

Mai Gumbo ended the call. She was upset that Rose's mum had cut short the conversation. Now she was baying for the blood of Pastor Nehemiah and Rose.

***

Pastor Nehemiah and Rose finished packing their luggage and hired a taxi to the airport. 'Thank you for the nice time. I really enjoyed the quality time with you.' Rose kissed him. He smooched her.

She squeezed his hand and laid her head on his chest in the departure lounge. She kissed him. Rose had enjoyed their shenanigans. She now wished for more happy times ahead. He had demonstrated his affection for her.

3

Pastor Nehemiah and Rose sauntered side by side into the arrivals hall at Robert Mugabe International Airport.

A surge of rage overwhelmed Mai Gumbo when she saw them together. She charged at them and pounced like a raging lioness.

'How dare you steal my husband?' Mai Gumbo punched Rose in the cheek, knocking her down.

'How dare you spend $10 000 of our savings on this whore?' She slapped Pastor Nehemiah across the face. He fell on the ground. 'How dare you!'

Mai Gumbo was frothing on the mouth and going berserk. She charged at Rose again, but she was restrained by airport security staff before she could land another blow on her. Rose cowered from her, petrified.

'Please calm down, I will explain everything,' Pastor Nehemiah pleaded with Mai Gumbo.

'I don't need any explanations from you. You are a lying, shameless cheat.' Mai Gumbo tried to slap him, and he dodged her.

There was commotion inside the arrivals hall with onlookers gaping at Mai Gumbo yelling obscenities at Pastor Nehemiah and Rose. She was dragged away by airport security staff.

'Are you alright, madam?' one of the security staff asked Rose. 'Do you wish to press charges of assault?'

Rose shook her head and pressed a tissue on her bleeding nose. She hired a taxi and was whisked away.

Pastor Nehemiah apologised to the airport security staff for Mai Gumbo's violent conduct and begged them to release her. He was embarrassed by the whole incident.

Eventually, the officer in charge of security cautioned Mai Gumbo against causing any more assaults in the airport. She was now as calm as a wet hen. A church driver took them home. The drive home was quiet, except for Mai Gumbo's sobs.

***

'Can you please tell me the truth? Why are you having an affair with Pastor Nehemiah, a married man?' Mum repositioned herself on the hospital bed and glared at Rose.

'I am not.'

'How come the pastor's wife called me alleging that you were having an affair with her husband? Tell me the truth, Rose. What is going on? Aren't there single and eligible bachelors in the church? Why cheat with a married man, of all people?'

'There is nothing going on between us.'

'You lied to me that you were going on a school trip, but you were playing hanky panky in Cape Town. What has got into you, Rose?'

'Nothing,' Rose was getting annoyed by the interrogation.

Mum was very visibly upset. 'Tell me, why, Rose?'

'You want to know the truth. Can you handle the truth? The truth hurts, mum. Sorry, mum, that I fell short of your expectations. But I had no other option, you are all I have, and you were dying of cancer. What was I supposed to do? Pastor Nehemiah offered me money in exchange of engaging in an affair with him. I didn't want to see you die. So, I agreed to having an affair with him, so that I could save you from dying.'

Mum glared at her speechless.

'I am so sorry, mum.'

'I want you to stop fornicating with Pastor Nehemiah. And you must also stop attending his church immediately. Didn't I warn you about attending these dodgy churches with pastors who bamboozle gullible believers with many social problems, to part with their hard-earned cash, and they abuse young women like you? These are shameless charlatans.'

'I will stop seeing him.'

'You must do so immediately.'

'What happened to your face? It's swollen.'

'I fell in the bathtub.'

Rose was relieved that she didn't tell mum about the assault at the airport. Mum would have had a heart attack. She returned to her flat.

***

'I will sue Rose for damages for cheating with you,' said Mai Gumbo. 'What is it she has that I don't have? Tell me, aren't I a woman too?'

'I am so sorry. Please forgive me,' Pastor Nehemiah knelt before Mai Gumbo in the bedroom.

'Get up. I don't trust you anymore. Why did you defile the sanctity of our marriage?'

'I am so sorry.'

'You must immediately get counselling from Pastor Dimba. You must repent of your carnal desires. Aren't you ashamed of preying on the single young woman?'

'We must protect the reputation of our church.'

'What about the reputation of our marriage? I don't care about the church's reputation. You must pay for your infidelity.'

'Please forgive me. I won't do it again.'

'I'm not yet ready to forgive you. From now onwards, you must sleep in the spare bedroom. I can't stand the sight of your filthy body sleeping beside me.'

Mai Gumbo threw blankets at him.

Pastor Nehemiah picked up the blankets and walked off to the spare bedroom. Mai Gumbo sobbed all night.

Pastor Nehemiah couldn't sleep either. He dreaded the news of his infidelity spreading in and outside the church. This would do irreparable reputational damage to his ministry. He had worked hard over a long time to build this ministry. He had to do damage limitation. But how would he do damage limitation when his wife was threatening to bring him down?

4

The following day, Pastor Nehemiah phoned Rose informing her that their affair was now over. He had to save his marriage. He informed her that Mai Gumbo intended to take legal action against her. 'You must stop attending church at the moment so that you don't inflame the situation,' he said.

'I didn't intend to return there anyway. I will defend myself in court. I'm not a homewrecker. You coerced me into the affair,' Rose countered.

'I will compensate you if you agree to sign a non-disclosure agreement. This means you must not disclose our affair to the press. It's a win-win situation.'

'You are a pervert preying on vulnerable single church women. I don't want your compensation. I want to expose you instead.'

'You and I had a consensual affair. Don't even bother going to the police and making false allegations. They won't listen to your nonsense. I know the Police Commissioner. He is my friend.' Pastor Nehemiah raised his voice in anger.

'You messed with the wrong woman, Mr. Man of God. I will sue you for rape and bring you down,' Rose was spewing verbal acid over the phone.

'Move on, Rose. There is plenty fish in the sea,' Pastor Nehemiah said calmly.

'How can I just move on, when I am pregnant?'

'What! But you said you were using contraceptive pills? You must terminate this pregnancy.'

'I won't do that. I want the whole world to know that you fathered my baby.'

'Are you blackmailing me now? I know a good doctor who provides a discreet abortion service. And I will pay for the service and increase your compensation. No one should know about our affair. It will destroy my reputation and everything that I worked so hard to build.'

'I don't want your compensation. I will keep my baby and raise it on my own.'

'What do you want then? Just don't dare sell the story of our affair to the press. I will sue you for defamation.'

'I will do just that,' Rose ended the call.

***

'It is wonderful to see you again, my dear brother, in Christ. It's been a long time,' Pastor Dimba drew out a chair for Pastor Nehemiah. 'You sounded desperate on the phone. What brings you to my office at such short notice?'

Pastor Nehemiah cleared his throat. 'Well, I sinned, dear brother.'

'We are all sinners who have fallen short of the glory of God.'

'I have been fornicating with a young woman, Rose, from the church and my dear wife, Mai Gumbo, discovered the affair. Hell has no fury like a jilted pastor's wife.'

Pastor Dimba was shocked. He said a short prayer.

There was a pause. Pastor Dimba gazed at Pastor Nehemiah like a therapist. 'Why Man of God?'

Pastor Nehemiah narrated how he developed an infatuation with Rose and started the affair with her three months earlier. But Mai Gumbo had discovered the affair and caused a scene at Robert Gabriel Mugabe International

Airport. He said he needed to save his marriage. So, he needed guidance and counselling on healing his marriage and repentance.

'What triggered your affair with Rose?'

'I had sexual intimacy issues with Mai Gumbo.'

'Did you talk to her about the issue?'

'Yes, I did.'

'And what did she say?'

'She dismissed my concerns on lack of intimacy on the marriage bed. She was not interested in that talk. Her libido seems to have gone down. But she didn't listen to me. I have the libido of a bull. So, I started the affair. I needed a bit by the side.'

'So, you thought cheating was a means to an end?'

'Yes. Besides, Rose is very gorgeous. I couldn't resist the temptation.'

'That is a serious sin. You sinned before God and broke the heart of the wife that you swore before heaven and earth to love and hold, in health and sickness, till death parted you.'

Pastor Dimba opened his bible. He read Ephesians 5v 25. He explained the duty of husbands to love their wives as they love their bodies and not defile the sanctity of marriage.

'I understand that.'

'Take a moment to critically reflect on the impact of your infidelity on your wife, your reputation and your congregation.'

'Mai Gumbo is so heartbroken. She won't even talk to me. We now sleep in separate bedrooms.'

'I understand the pain she feels because of your infidelity.'

'I am really sorry for cheating on her.'

'Being sorry is not enough. You must express genuine repentance before God and restore the trust and lost love in your marriage.'

Pastor Nehemiah began to weep.

'Take some time away from preaching for weeks and pray earnestly, seeking repentance from the Lord. You have to demonstrate to your wife, in words and deeds, that you are remorseful and seeking to heal the wounds caused by your infidelity. We will meet again soon for another counselling session.'

'Thank you.' Pastor Nehemiah stood up and left the office.

5

Rose read the story of the trial of Harvey Weinstein on her tablet. She felt sympathy for the women who took him to court for abuse and were revictimised through the media scrutiny and cross examination in court by the defence team.

Rose wasn't sure she had the guts to stand up in court before a magistrate. She wished there was a way to make him pay for the abuse of power and trust.

Rose pondered whether to leak her story to the press. The story would damage Pastor Nehemiah's reputation. The press would scramble for the juicy story of a famous city Pastor who cheated on his wife with a congregant and impregnated her. But was she ready to face Pastor Nehemiah's lawyers in a defamation case?

Rose was dying for revenge on him, for using her and then dumping her. She wanted to shatter the façade and expose his real personality to the world. Eventually, the desire for vengeance overwhelmed her. Rose picked the phone and called the editor's desk at The Herald daily, a national newspaper.

She said she was the elder sister of a woman who had been having an affair with Pastor Nehemiah. Now, her sister was pregnant, and she wanted to warn other women to stay away from the abuser, Pastor Nehemiah Gumbo.

***

The following day, *The Herald* newspaper carried a front-page headline of a famous city pastor who had allegedly been having an extra marital affair with an unnamed single woman in the church, who was now pregnant. The story was based on an unnamed source.

'Did you leak the story of our affair to the press?' Pastor Nehemiah interrogated Rose over the phone.

'No, I didn't.'

'It must be you. You are such a vindictive bitch. If it turns out that you leaked the story to the press, I will sue you for defamation.'

'I have nothing to do with the leaked story. Someone else leaked it.'

'Reporters from The Herald have been phoning my office asking me for a comment,' said Pastor Nehemiah.

'Please leave me alone. Stop phoning or texting me. You and I are done.' Rose ended the call.

Rose started receiving anonymous, threatening text messages on her WhatsApp account. She blocked the text messages.

Mum phoned later that afternoon. She blamed Rose for not listening to her warning not to attend the new churches mushrooming in the city.

'No point in crying over spilled milk, mum. You must support me just as I have supported you through your cancer treatment.'

There was a momentary silence. 'You must learn from your mistakes, Rose.'

'Yes, mum. Good day.' Rose ended the call.

6

That afternoon, Rose visited Madzimai Trust and met Amy, a support worker. She narrated how she had been coerced into a relationship by married Pastor Nehemiah and she needed advice on what to do next.

Amy said she had worked on many cases involving abuse of vulnerable single women by church pastors. She showed her statistics of the prevalence of sexual abuse inside the church.

Amy said there were more victims of abuse in the church, but they found it difficult to come forward and report their abuse for fear of not being believed or they were paid off to keep quiet about the abuse. She cited a previous case, where an alleged victim had withdrawn her complaint after she received compensation from an unnamed pastor and was forced to sign a non-disclosure agreement.

'What should I do then?' Rose asked.

'You could take legal action to stop Pastor Nehemiah from abusing more women in the church.'

'But it's his word against mine. Will the police and judge believe me?'

'We provide counselling and free legal advice from one of our pro bono female lawyers. Think about it and let me know what you decide to do next.'

Suddenly, Rose began to cry.

'What is the matter? Did I say something to upset you?'

'No. I am pregnant.'

'Lord, no! And it's Pastor Nehemiah's?'

'Yes.'

'Are you going to have an abortion?'

'I don't know.'

'I know an old woman who can help you terminate the pregnancy. That is if you decide to do so.'

'I haven't made up my mind yet.'

***

Rose was strolling in the city centre heading towards the commuter omnibus rank when she bumped into Chengetai.

'Where have you been? I haven't seen you for a while, Chengetai,' Rose shook her hand.

'I left Paradise Life Ministries Church.'

'Why?'

'Well, Pastor Nehemiah forced himself on me inside his office at the church.'

'Did you report the incident to the church leadership or the police?'

'I reported the incident to the church leadership. They didn't thoroughly investigate the incident and they doubted my version of events. I didn't think the police would believe me either. So, I left the church in frustration.'

'I am so sorry, Chengetai.'

'More women were abused by Pastor Nehemiah in the church and the leaders knew about it. But they did nothing to safeguard us. Apparently, Pastor Nehemiah thinks he is untouchable.'

'He must be stopped.'

'Did he abuse you too, Rose?'

'Yes. But I am not backing down quietly. I will stop him. Would you be willing to stand in court and share your witness statement of that incident at the hands of Pastor Nehemiah?'

'I don't know about that. I have moved on with my life and I am now engaged to a good man.'

Rose and Chengetai swapped mobile phone numbers.

'Thank you, Chengetai. I will contact you sometime. It was high time the wolf in sheep skin was exposed and punished for abusing vulnerable, single church women.'

They hugged and parted ways.

7

The following morning, Rose phoned Amy and informed her that she would take legal action against Pastor Nehemiah.

Amy reassured her that she had made the right decision to stop further abuse of women by Pastor Nehemiah. She organised an afternoon meeting with Rose and Yvonne, a female lawyer working pro bono with survivors of abuse at Madzimai Trust.

***

That afternoon, Amy introduced Rose to Yvonne, a young, tall, beautiful, well-dressed lawyer who didn't smile.

'How long did you have an affair with Pastor Nehemiah?' Yvonne asked.

'Three months.'

'Let's get this clear, were you sexually abused by Pastor Nehemiah, or you engaged in a consensual relationship with him?'

'He coerced me into a relationship when I was emotionally vulnerable, and my mum had just been diagnosed with cancer.'

'I believe you, Rose. But the defence won't. They will cross examine the nature of your relationship with Pastor Nehemiah. You must stick to your story.'

Rose wasn't impressed by Yvonne's direct and cold questioning. She doubted whether she would work well with her.

'You must first file a rape case allegation against Pastor Nehemiah at the charge office.'

***

'Have you considered what will happen when you sue a famous and powerful *Man of God* like Pastor Nehemiah?' mum gazed at Rose. 'Your court story will be splashed all over the daily newspapers and you will be accused of trying to bring him down. Your reputation is also at stake. Think twice, Rose.'

'But, mum, he forced himself on me and other women. He must be stopped.'

'Didn't I tell you not to attend these dodgy city churches, in the first place? But you put twigs in your ears. Look what's happened now.'

'Anyway, I will go ahead without your support, mum. You don't care, do you? I have the support of Amy and Yvonne and other survivors of abuse.'

'Are you now questioning my love for you, Rose? After all the sacrifices I have made raising you as a single mum. Isn't that love? All I am saying is there is a huge price to pay for facing up to such a famous, powerful, and well-connected man like Pastor Nehemiah in court.'

'I am ready to face him and have my day in court.'

'Good luck then,' mum said half-heartedly.

***

Rose went alone to the police station to file a rape case against Pastor Nehemiah. Amy and Yvonne couldn't be available to escort her. She mustered courage and entered the charge office.

'How may I help you, madam?' asked a male police officer at the reception.

'Can I please speak to a female police officer? I wish to file a complaint.' Rose hesitated.

'Sorry, we don't have a female office on duty,' replied the officer. 'We've only got male officers. What is the complaint?'

'Can we speak in private?'

'I will deal with your complaint. Please follow me.'

The male officer led Rose to an empty interview room. He shuffled his forms and looked at her. 'What is your complaint, madam?'

'I was abused by a prominent church pastor in the city. I want him charged.'

'Abused? How?'

'He raped me.'

'Raped?'

'Yes.'

'Who raped you?'

'Pastor Nehemiah Gumbo.' The officer's mouth gaped.

'This is a serious allegation against the Man of God. Tell me, did you have an affair with him?'

'Yes.'

'So, you are trying to get even with him after the affair ended?'

'No. He forced himself on me over three months.'

'Why didn't you file a complaint the first time he raped you?'

'Because he was coercively controlling.'

The officer looked at Rose's face like a psychic. 'Let us pause the interview for a minute,' the officer exited the interview room quickly. Rose wondered why he had left in a hurry. Minutes later the officer returned.

'How many times did Pastor Nehemiah force himself on you?'

'Five times.'

'And you didn't file a complaint during those times? It appears that you two were involved in a consensual adult affair. Why are you tarnishing the image of Pastor Nehemiah?'

'Because he is a predator who preys on vulnerable, single women in the church. And I expect you, as a police officer, to listen, protect and safeguard me from this predator. Instead, you are not willing to help me. I will file my rape complaint with your superiors.'

'You don't have to go to my superiors to file this matter. I will finish filing the docket and I will do the initial investigations.'

By the time the interview ended, Rose was tired of the interrogation. She realised it would be an uphill task to convince a male magistrate that the revered man of God, Pastor Nehemiah, abused her. But she was determined to have her day in court. A burning desire for justice crackled inside her mind like a fire.

Part Three

1

Paradise Life Ministries Pentecostal Church leadership issued a press statement denying the rape allegations against Pastor Nehemiah. The statement supported Pastor Nehemiah and outlined the safeguarding policies and procedures inside the church.

Rose was disgusted when she read the press statement. She would have her day in court and prove that Pastor Nehemiah was a wolf behind the pulpit. But she was afraid that her credibility would be attacked by the defence lawyers and Pastor Nehemiah's supporters. She phoned Yvonne about the press statement.

Yvonne wasn't too bothered about the statement and dismissed it as a gimmick of a church defending its founder Pastor Nehemiah and it bad reputation. She advised Rose to focus on reading her court statement instead.

Rose complained about the Facebook trolls labelling her 'a manipulative liar bent on bringing down the anointed Man of God.'

Yvonne reminded her that no one could police what people said on Facebook, and this was expected behaviour from Pastor Nehemiah's faithful followers.

Rose noted how she was angered by false online gossip, and she wanted to respond to it. But Yvonne warned her against making comments in response to social media trolls because this would add fuel to fire and jeopardise the impending trial. She reminded Rose that she would have her day in court.

Rose was frustrated by Yvonne's indifference to the social media trolling. She suggested that Yvonne should issue a press statement setting the record straight about the rape allegations she was making against Pastor Nehemiah. Yvonne agreed to issue a press statement.

***

Meanwhile, Pastor Nehemiah appeared on his weekly church radio broadcast dismissing the rape allegations against him by Rose as 'the wiles of the devil.' He said he was unfazed by the rape allegations and accused Rose of being an evil woman, 'Jezebel'. He prophesied that the court would acquit him.

He urged his followers to pray and fast for him, so that he would overcome this trial by fire. His ardent supporters phoned into the show expressing their solidarity with him and pledging their unwavering support. Pastor Nehemiah was delighted by the outpouring of support.

Pastor Nehemiah encouraged his supporters to come in huge numbers to the trial to demonstrate solidarity with him.

The supporters donated funds to hire the services of Mr. Mudzi, one of the best high profile trial lawyers in the city.

***

Rose began dreading the impending trial. She felt imposter syndrome and doubted if she could stand a chance against Pastor Nehemiah in court. The social media vitriol from Pastor Nehemiah's supporters made her start to doubt herself.

On certain days, Rose wished the ground could just open and swallow her. She dreaded cross examination in court.

However, on other days, she felt a determination to testify in court against Pastor Nehemiah Gumbo, the wolf hiding behind the pulpit and preying on vulnerable single women.

One day, Rose called Amy on her mobile phone. 'I am not sure I have the guts to face Pastor Nehemiah in court.'

'Why are you getting cold feet? Be strong because you are doing the right thing, Rose. Pastor Nehemiah must be stopped. Or else he will continue to abuse more vulnerable women while the church leadership turns a blind eye. You are our only hope to stop this predator. Don't let us down.'

'I'm starting to doubt myself. Someone described me on social media as, "a manipulative, gold digger tarnishing the good name of the anointed Man of God."

'I will support you all the way. Stay strong, Rose.' Amy said calmly on the phone.

'Thank you,' Rose sighed. She ended the call and felt relieved.

Yvonne issued a press statement, in The Herald newspaper the following day, emphasising that Rose was a victim of sexual abuse by perpetrator Pastor Nehemiah, and she would prove the rape allegations in the real court, not in the court of public opinion.

The statement also described Pastor Nehemiah as 'a wolf hiding behind the pulpit and abusing his position of trust by preying on vulnerable single women in his church. Now the wolf had been unmasked.'

2

The media buzz about the trial divided public opinion. Some people felt that there was no real case against Pastor Nehemiah because he was a middle-aged stud sowing his wild oats and engaged in a consensual adult relationship with Rose. They accused the 'woke brigade' of going too far. They accused Rose of being a gold digger and home wrecker.

However, women's rights activists came out in full support of Rose. They felt that the abuse of women in churches was an important issue that needed to be exposed and addressed.

The women's rights activists accused churches of not enforcing proper safeguarding policies and procedures to protect vulnerable single women from predatory pastors. They argued that Pastor Nehemiah was a case in point, because he abused his position of trust and should be held accountable in a court of law.

More support for Rose came from the ruling party's Women's League. They pledged continued support for vulnerable single women until the city was wiped clean of false prophets and charlatans that were abusing the women.

But Rose's mum was worried about the impact of bad press on Rose and the family name. Rose assured her that she had the support of other women, and that the trial would set a precedent on safeguarding vulnerable women in the churches.

Rose was emboldened by the outpouring support. But inside her psyche she was petrified. She was happy when mum eventually pledged to stand with her.

***

On the first day of the trial, Pastor Nehemiah arrived at court in a convoy of expensive cars. He was given a hero's welcome by multitudes of cheering church supporters full of pomp and holding placards bearing messages of support.

Rose and Yvonne, her lawyer, were greeted by a small group of vociferous women's rights activists holding placards of sisterly solidarity, outside court. Rose was jeered by Pastor Nehemiah's ardent supporters as she walked up the steps at Rotten Row Magistrate's Court main entrance. She feared a physical attack. Yvonne gripped her hand tightly and made a victory sign to the group of women's rights activists.

***

During the opening statement, in court, Yvonne stated that she would present evidence to the court showing that Rose was a victim of a sexual predator, Pastor Nehemiah, who coerced her into a relationship by lavishing her with money and gifts. She said Rose had also been physically assaulted by Mai Gumbo at Robert Mugabe International Airport.

Yvonne also stated that she would also show the court threatening text messages sent by Pastor Nehemiah to Rose after he discovered that she was pregnant. He had tried to coerce her into having an abortion. But she refused.

Mr. Mudzi, the defence lawyer, said that he would prove that Pastor Nehemiah was a good family Man of God whose name was being dragged through the mud by Rose, a vindictive woman. He dismissed the rape allegations as baseless and asserted that Rose and Pastor Nehemiah had been in a consensual affair.

Mr. Mudzi also accused Rose of tarnishing the good image of Paradise Life Ministries Church. He pledged to bring forward witnesses to testify about the good character of Pastor

Nehemiah and show the court the safeguarding policies and procedures in the church.

The magistrate, a middle-aged man, with a bald head, stated that the case would be heard over four days and judgement would be on the fifth day. He adjourned the day's proceedings.

***

The following morning, Rose took to the witness stand. Yvonne asked Rose how she had got entangled with Pastor Nehemiah of Paradise Life Church.

Rose explained how Pastor Nehemiah and Paradise Life Church members had been friendly and welcoming the first time she visited the church on a Sunday service. But things changed after she sought counselling from Pastor Nehemiah when her mother was diagnosed with cancer.

Pastor Nehemiah had made unwanted advances. She was baffled by his behaviour because she looked up to him as a mentor and father figure.

Yvonne asked why she didn't refuse the unwanted advances nor report the behaviour to the church leadership immediately.

Rose replied that Pastor Nehemiah was a manipulative man who preyed on her vulnerabilities.

Yvonne then asked how Pastor Nehemiah did that.

Rose said Pastor Nehemiah offered her money to pay for her mother's treatment and began to come to her flat uninvited and lavished her with expensive perfumes. She found it hard to resist the advances of such a determined, powerful Man of God. He had even coerced her to go to Cape Town with him.

Yvonne asked if she ever felt guilty and remorseful about being in the affair with a married man.

Rose said she felt guilty about the affair, and she wanted out. But he had dragged her deeper into the complicated love triangle. She didn't want to be a homewrecker.

Yvonne asked why she was suing Pastor Nehemiah when she had engaged in an affair with him.

Rose said it was because Pastor Nehemiah was a predator pastor who had caused her emotional distress and abused other vulnerable single women in his church. Therefore, he must be stopped before further abuses of more women.

***

That afternoon, Mr. Mudzi looked Rose in the eye. 'Why did you seek counselling from Pastor Nehemiah specifically, when there were other pastors in the church?'

'Because he was approachable,' Rose shifted in the witness box. Her voice had a tinge of nervousness.

'So, you went for counselling to an approachable man, whom you now label a predator. Why?'

'I didn't know him that well at first. I thought he was an honest and trustworthy person. Looks can be deceiving. Later I realised that he hid his predatory instincts behind a façade.'

'But you still went ahead and had an affair with him anyway?'

'Yes.'

'Why? Remember you are in the witness box.'

'I couldn't disentangle myself from him because he was so coercively controlling. He had the tentacles of an octopus.'

Mr. Mudzi laughed. 'So, you expect the court to accept your blatant lies, that you were a rape victim when you willingly engaged in the affair and lived a lavish lifestyle funded by Pastor Nehemiah? You are a gold digger. Now that the affair is over, you dragged this poor, fallible man of God to court because he couldn't keep it in his pants. Isn't that so?'

'No.'

'You were Pastor Nehemiah's bit by the side, his 'small house.' Isn't that so?'

'Suit yourself.' Rose frowned.

Someone in the audience laughed.

The magistrate ordered silence in his court.

'Your honour, Mr. Mudzi is shoving words into my client's mouth,' Yvonne protested.

'Rose is tarnishing the good name of Pastor Nehemiah and his church. She must be thoroughly cross examined. She shouldn't throw stones when she lives in a glass apartment.' Mr. Mudzi paused.

'Proceed,' the magistrate gestured to him.

'Describe the first time you had sexual intercourse with Pastor Nehemiah,' Mr. Mudzi stood close to Rose and eyed her suspiciously.

'He coerced me to dinner in a restaurant at Rainbow Towers.'

'Did you enjoy the dinner?'

'Wasn't a bad experience.'

'Did you have plenty to drink?'

'One glass of wine.'

Mr. Mudzi turned to the magistrate. 'May the court put on record that the complainant, Rose, didn't drink too much to be deemed incapable of giving consent to sex.'

Rose described how after the dinner, Pastor Nehemiah had taken her to her flat and they had ended up having sexual intercourse in bed.

'Did you report to the police that Pastor Nehemiah had raped you that night?'

'No.'

'Why not?'

'I was very confused. I didn't think anyone would believe me.'

'But you continued with the affair with him?'

'Yes.'

'Why?'

'My client was taken advantage of, your honour,' Yvonne interjected. 'Abuse victims end up in a state of learned helplessness.'

'I don't think hers was a case of learned helplessness, your honour. She was a willing participant,' countered Mr. Mudzi. 'Rose enjoyed the tango with Pastor Nehemiah and the benefits of that affair. No further questions, your honour.'

Yvonne stood up. 'Your honour, victims of intimate partner abuse have strategies of coping with the abuse. Rose is a victim of the nefarious behaviour of Pastor Nehemiah who hides behind the pulpit, and preys on vulnerable single women in the Church. The Court should listen to the voice of the victim here, Rose.'

'Yes, my court is listening to Rose's voice,' said the magistrate. 'Proceed.'

Yvonne told the court that Rose was a victim of emotional and physical abuse by Pastor Nehemiah. She also cited the physical assault of Rose at the Robert Mugabe International Airport by Mai Gumbo. Yvonne sat down.

Mr. Mudzi stood up and showed the court images of Rose and Pastor Nehemiah at the beach in Cape Town. 'Can you explain why you, a victim of abuse, are seen in these photos cosying with your abuser, my client, in a floral bikini by the beach in Cape Town?'

'He enticed me to wear a bikini to the beach. He said I looked sexy.'

'Why are you lying about your steamy shenanigans with Pastor Nehemiah?' Mr. Mudzi shook his head.

'I am not lying.' Rose screwed her face.

'You are. You are a manipulative liar. I hope the court sees through your veil of lies.' Mr. Mudzi sat down.

Rose was tired and emotionally drained after the cross examination. Tears glistened like gems in her eyes. She was relieved when the magistrate adjourned the proceedings.

Yvonne patted Rose on the shoulder and commended her for withstanding the barrage of questions from Mr. Mudzi.

3

On the second day of court proceedings, Yvonne brought forward a new witness, a woman who was a former church secretary at Paradise Life Ministries Church.

Mr. Mudzi approached the Magistrate's desk. 'Your honour, the witness, Stella, can't testify in court because she reached an out of court settlement with Pastor Nehemiah and signed a non-disclosure agreement.'

'But your honour, Stella has been brave to come forward to testify about the pervert, Pastor Nehemiah,' said Yvonne. 'She saw the court story in the newspaper.'

'Here is the non-disclosure agreement, your honour.' Mr. Mudzi handed the signed contract to him.

The magistrate studied the agreement. 'I will not allow the witness to testify in my court because she was paid compensation and agreed to the terms of the non-disclosure agreement.'

Yvonne shook her head and threw her hands in the air. She was visibly disappointed.

Rose returned to the witness stand. Yvonne gazed at her and smiled. 'Yesterday, you said Pastor Nehemiah was coercively controlling. In what ways?'

'He forced me to wear what he wanted for dinner and pressured me into having sex and going to Cape Town with him and wearing a bikini on the beach.'

'Why didn't you challenge his controlling behaviour?'

'He is a complicated person; kind, persuasive, manipulative and controlling.'

'No further questions, your honour.' Yvonne sat down.

Mr. Mudzi stood up. 'He forced you to wear a bikini on the beach.' He laughed. 'The pictures of you two love doves at the beach, paint a different picture of two adults in a consensual affair. Your honour, I move that the court dismisses these spurious allegations against my client, Pastor Nehemiah.'

The magistrate gazed at him with a blank expression on his face.

Mr. Mudzi insisted that the magistrate must disregard the accusations against Pastor Nehemiah. He accused Rose of jumping on the bandwagon of woke feminists who brought down powerful men like Harvey Weinstein. He urged the magistrate not to be sidetracked by Rose who was a member of the Me-Too movement.

Yvonne stood up and asked the magistrate to stop Mr. Mudzi from making unfounded accusations about Rose's involvement with the Me-Too movement, because this was not the issue on trial in the court.

The magistrate looked at his watch. He adjourned the trial for the following day.

Outside court, Stella, the woman who had been barred from taking the witness stand, spoke to Yvonne and Rose. 'I know another woman who was abused by Pastor Nehemiah and the church leaders didn't thoroughly investigate her alleged abuse case. Her name is Chengetai.'

Rose knew about Chengetai but didn't admit to knowing her. Stella gave Chengetai's number to Yvonne.

That evening, Yvonne phoned Chengetai. She didn't answer her phone. Yvonne left a voicemail message on her phone. Chengetai returned the call.

Initially, Chengetai refused to come and testify against Pastor Nehemiah because she had moved on with her life after the abuse incident and she didn't want the media spotlight.

But Yvonne persuaded her to come to court and testify so that she could find closure to her trauma of abuse and protect other vulnerable women who might be abused by Pastor Nehemiah.

Eventually, Chengetai agreed to appear in court, as a witness, the following morning. Yvonne thanked her.

***

That night, Brother Kudakwashe from the church choir phoned Rose. He asked her how she was coping with the trial. Rose said she was fine. Brother Kudakwashe informed her that Pastor Nehemiah had taken time off his preaching duties, in order to reflect, repent and attend the trial. Mai Gumbo and the children had stopped attending church regularly. And there was grapevine that Mai Gumbo intended to move out of the marital home with the children, and file for divorce.

There were now two factions vying for power inside the church. One faction wanted Pastor Nehemiah removed from his senior pastor position in the church because he had tarnished the image of the church.

While the other faction wanted Pastor Nehemiah to return to his pastoral duties after seeking repentance for the extra marital affair.

Brother Kudakwashe wished Rose well during the trial. She thanked him for the call.

Rose wondered why Brother Kudakwashe was calling her now. *Did he break up with Maidei and was he checking her out?* Rose didn't want anything to do with men at the moment.

Rose received more messages of support from different women's rights organisations in Harare, encouraging her to soldier on in the trial. She was overwhelmed by the outpouring of support and wrote down her feelings of joy and gratitude in her diary.

4

On the third day of court proceedings, Chengetai was late for court. Yvonne begged the impatient magistrate to delay proceedings by 15 minutes until Chengetai, a key prosecution witness, arrived. The magistrate agreed begrudgingly. He said the defence lawyer would proceed with his cross examination of Rose if Chengetai didn't arrive on time.

Yvonne thanked the magistrate. She gazed impatiently at the door, for Chengetai. *Did Chengetai change her mind about testifying? Did something happen to her?* Yvonne phoned Chengetai but her phone was switched off.

Two minutes before the 15-minute deadline, Chengetai strolled into the magistrate's court. Yvonne was relieved. She asked Chengetai why she had been late for court. Chengetai said the commuter omnibus had burst a tyre on the way and so she had to hitchhike into town. Her phone had run out of battery.

Yvonne thanked her for coming.

Chengetai took to the witness stand and described how Pastor Nehemiah had been very friendly to her at first, and she had trusted him as her pastor and a father figure.

Then one day Pastor Nehemiah invited her into his office. He told her that he was attracted to her. Chengetai was shocked and replied that she couldn't engage in an affair with him because he was married and her pastor.

Pastor Nehemiah had caressed Chengetai on the shoulder. She stood back and was ready to leave. But he blocked her way. He lunged at her, and she had cowered into the corner of the office. He forced a kiss on her mouth and fondled her breasts. Chengetai had screamed at him to stop it. But he had laughed instead. She tried to force her way past him. But he gripped her hands and kissed her again. She had wrestled out of his grip and bolted out of his office. She went home petrified and crying.

The court was silent as she described the harrowing incident.

Chengetai shed tears as she described the impact of the incident on her mental and emotional wellbeing and relationship with men.

Mr. Mudzi gazed at Chengetai. 'Did you report the incident to church leadership or the police?'

'Yes, to the church leadership.'

'What did they do?'

'They said it was difficult for them to investigate because there were no other witnesses, and it was my word against Pastor Nehemiah's. Instead, the church leaders blamed me for having a crush on Pastor Nehemiah and fabricating the story.'

'Why didn't you report this alleged abuse incident to the police?'

'When the church leadership refused to properly investigate the abuse incident, I was so disheartened, and I decided not to report the case to the police. I didn't think they would believe me either.'

'Why should the court believe you now when the church leadership didn't believe your version of the alleged abuse incident?' Mr. Mudzi had a stern look on his face.

'Because what I am saying is true.'

'Are you friends with Rose?'

'No. We were church mates and served briefly in the choir together.'

Mr. Mudzi glared at Chengetai. 'It appears that you have joined Rose's bandwagon trying to bring down the revered Man of God. That plot won't work. Pastor Nehemiah denies that the incident ever happened.' He rested his case. The trial was adjourned for the afternoon.

***

That afternoon Mr. Mudzi brought a middle-aged woman, a church member, to testify about Pastor Nehemiah's good character. The woman said that she was thankful that Pastor Nehemiah had brought her to the Lord when she was addicted to alcohol and was involved in prostitution. She said she would have died had the Man of God not preached the words of repentance to her. She said he was a good family man and the rape allegations made by Rose were false.

'How well do you know Pastor Nehemiah's private life and shenanigans with vulnerable single women?' Yvonne stood up and asked her.

'I don't know much about his private life.'

'So, how can you testify that he is not guilty of the rape allegations when you don't know him that well? He is a wolf in sheep skin preying on vulnerable single women. He is a pervert hiding behind a façade.'

The witness shook her head. 'I don't think so.'

Yvonne asked what she thought might be the motives of Rose and Chengetai testifying against Pastor Nehemiah.

She said she didn't know.

Afterwards, Mai Gumbo took to the witness stand and testified for her husband, Pastor Nehemiah. She said Rose was making false accusations against her husband.

'Why should she and Chengetai make false accusations against your husband?' Yvonne asked.

'He is pastoring a mega church in Harare, and they are jealous of his thriving ministry, so they want to bring him down.'

Yvonne laughed and addressed the court. 'This is serious case of abuse of position of trust and sexual abuse by Pastor Nehemiah. The court must find him guilty.'

Mai Gumbo shook her head. 'My husband is not guilty of abuse.' Yvonne rested her case.

'Is all well in your marriage?' Mr. Mudzi stood up and approached Mai Gumbo.

'Our marriage, like all marriages, has its challenges. But we are working at healing the pain caused by the alleged infidelity of my husband. He is getting counselling from his mentor, Pastor Dimba.'

'How are you feeling when your husband is standing before the court, accused of sexual abuse, and not preaching in church?'

'I am sad and incredibly angry with my husband for failing to live up to the word that he preaches. I also feel a burning anger and hate for Rose, for making these false allegations. I feel betrayed by her because I let her in my house and our church, but now she is wrecking my marriage and destroying the image of our church.'

'Why did your husband get involved in the affair with Rose?'

'I don't know. Ask him. His weakness is that he is so trusting, and he is now paying for that.' Mr. Mudzi sat down. Mai Gumbo stepped out of the witness box.

Rose was recalled to the witness stand. 'Why did Pastor Nehemiah send you threatening WhatsApp messages?'

'Because I told him that I was pregnant.'

'Prostitute!' someone yelled in court.

'Order!' The magistrate asked the security to remove the person from his court.

Yvonne read out aloud the messages in which Pastor Nehemiah coerced Rose to have an abortion.

Rose shed tears as she explained the impact of the messages on her.

Yvonne paused and rested her case.

Mr. Mudzi stood up and studied Rose's facial expression. His face was cynical. 'Are you carrying Pastor Nehemiah's child?'

'Yes.'

He looked at the magistrate. 'Your honour, I request a pregnancy test.'

The magistrate looked at Rose. 'Do you consent to a pregnancy test?'

'Yes.'

The magistrate adjourned the proceedings and ordered that Rose have a pregnancy test. The court proceedings would resume the following morning.

That night Rose received an anonymous text message, 'You are up to your old dirty tricks again. This time we will get even.' She knew it was her ex-partner, Rodney. *Why was he contacting her now? What was he up to now?*

5

The test confirmed that Rose was pregnant. Yvonne emphasised that Rose was carrying Pastor Nehemiah's baby after he forced himself on her several times.

Mr. Mudzi disagreed. And he called another defence witness to the stand.

Rose froze when she saw the witness.

Mr. Mudzi introduced Mr. Rodney Nkomo, a local businessman. He said he knew Rose well and had previously had an affair with her.

'How long did you have the affair with Rose?'

'Two years.'

'What type of a person is Rose?'

'She is definitely a gorgeous young woman with a good eye for men with money.'

'Why did you come to testify?'

'I know that poor Pastor Nehemiah fell prey to the scheming Rose, a manipulative liar. I didn't want what happened to me to also happen to Pastor Nehemiah.'

'What happened to you?'

'Rose extorted money from me. She used fake HIV positive test results and accused me of giving her the virus. She threatened to go public about the test results and sue me. I didn't want my family to know about the affair and besides, the negative publicity would ruin my business reputation. So, I paid her $30 000 to buy her silence.'

Rodney showed the court a receipt and settlement statement signed by him and Rose.

The magistrate nodded and turned to Yvonne. 'Do you have questions for this witness?'

Yvonne stood up and approached Mr. Rodney Nkomo. 'How did you meet Rose?'

'She was in university, and I met her on campus. I became her blesser, her sugar daddy. I was relieved when the affair ended. And I reconciled with my wife.'

Yvonne peered into his eyes. 'Tell me the truth, Mr. Nkomo. Didn't you come forward to testify against Rose because you are jealous that she has moved on and you want to get even with her?'

'No.'

Yvonne addressed the magistrate, 'Your honour, can you disregard the testimony of Mr. Rodney Nkomo because it is not relevant to the rape allegations against Pastor Nehemiah. Besides, Mr. Nkomo is revictimising my client.'

'I will allow the testimony because it shows Rose's character,' said the magistrate.

'No further question, your honour.' Yvonne walked back to her chair and sat down.

The magistrate told the court that he would now go and examine all the evidence presented in court, and he would pass a judgement the following morning.

6

The following morning, the magistrate walked into the courthouse, and he glanced around. He beckoned to Mr. Mudzi. 'Where is your client?'

'Pastor Nehemiah has not yet arrived, your honour. And I can't get hold of him. He is not answering my calls.'

'Does your client know that he is in contempt of court? Have you contacted his wife or the church leaders about his whereabouts? He must be here now while I deliver my verdict.'

'His wife said he left home for court.'

The magistrate was furious, 'I will deliver my verdict in ten minutes. I will hold your client in contempt of court if he doesn't arrive within that time.'

Mr. Mudzi glanced at the door of the court, anticipating Pastor Nehemiah to walk through. But he didn't show up.

The magistrate cleared his throat and rearranged the papers in front of him. Then he addressed the court. 'After careful deliberation on the evidence presented in this case, I hereby find that the defendant, Pastor Nehemiah Gumbo abused his position of trust, as Senior Pastor of Paradise Life Church, and engaged in sexual relationship with the plaintiff, Rose. Pastors must be good shepherds. It is clear that Pastor Nehemiah was a bad shepherd and took advantage of Rose's vulnerability and coerced her into a sexual relationship. The testimony of Chengetai also showed that there was a pattern of abusive behaviour by Pastor Nehemiah. It is the duty of my court to safeguard vulnerable single women from abuse when the church leadership ignores their allegations of abuse. Therefore, I find Pastor Nehemiah guilty of rape.'

Someone yelled an obscenity. He was removed from the court.

The magistrate paused and drank a glass of water. Then he proceeded, 'I order the police to issue an immediate warrant of arrest on Pastor Nehemiah. He is also in contempt of court. The court will adjourn until Monday for sentencing.' The magistrate stood up and left the building.

There were murmurs of shocked disbelief by supporters of Pastor Nehemiah.

Yvonne stood up and hugged Rose. 'We did it!' 'We did it, Rose!' Yvonne ejaculated, overwhelmed by emotion. She could hardly contain her euphoric self.

Rose wiped away tears. Yvonne held her hand and led her out of the crowded court.

'You shameless bitch!' one supporter of Pastor Nehemiah hurled insults at Rose.

Outside court, a small group of feminists cheered with Rose. Hordes of journalists were jostling for a comment.

'What is your comment on the verdict?' one tv journalist asked, blocking Rose and Yvonne's way.

Yvonne stopped and addressed the journalist. 'My client, Rose, is happy with the verdict. The magistrate delivered a good judgement that stops a wolf hiding behind the pulpit from preying on vulnerable single women in the church.'

'What do you have to say to other abusers and victims of abuse in the church?'

'My message is clear; to pastors, your days of abusing positions of trust in the church are over. The law will catch up with you if you abuse vulnerable single women,' Yvonne paused.

Then she continued, 'To the survivors of abuse, I say, be brave and come forward and tell your stories of experiencing abuse. The courts will listen to you. There has been a significant shift; courts are hearing more voices of survivors of abuse since the Harvey Weinstein case and the onset of the Me-Too movement.'

The magistrate's verdict headlined the radio and tv news bulletins. People discussed the whereabouts of the fugitive 'Man of God'. There were unsubstantiated claims that Pastor Nehemiah had fled to South Africa. The news media reported sightings of the convicted fugitive sexual predator pastor. The police warned the public to be vigilant and report any sightings of Pastor Nehemiah.

Inside her flat, Rose was relieved after the trial was over. She wanted to see Pastor Nehemiah locked away in prison. She also wanted to move on with her life.

***

The police searched for Pastor Nehemiah at the church and at his home. They couldn't find him. His family was worried about his safety and mental and emotional wellbeing. He was nowhere to be found.

Mai Gumbo assumed that he had fled to his rural home. She phoned her relatives and they said he wasn't there.

7

In the morning, Rose was making tea in the kitchen when she heard a hard knock on the flat door. She peeped through the peep hole. Her heart almost stopped beating when she saw Pastor Nehemiah standing outside, holding a gun.

She dashed through the lounge to her bedroom. She locked the bedroom door and barricaded the door with the bed. Rose trembled as she phoned the police. But no one was answering the phone.

'Open the door! I know you are in there! I will make you pay.' Pastor Nehemiah was banging hard on the door.

Rose called the police again. No one answered the call.

An alert neighbour heard the yelling and banging on the door, and he called the police.

Pastor Nehemiah broke down the door and forced himself into the flat. He headed for the bedroom.

Rose was shaking with fear like a cornered mouse. The call finally got through. 'Please hurry, he has broken into my flat. He is wielding a gun, like a mad man. He wants to shoot me.'

'Who is he?'

'Pastor Nehemiah.'

'You mean, Pastor Nehemiah, the fugitive pastor?'

'Yes.'

'What is your address madam?'

'Number one Roman Gardens on Second Street.'

'We are on our way.'

'Come out! You and I must get even.' Pastor Nehemiah was banging on the bedroom door. He tried to break through the barricaded door, but he couldn't. He smashed cups and saucers in a fit of rage. He heard the sound of police sirens in the distance and bolted out of the flat to his car. He sped off.

Two police officers rushed into Rose's flat. They wielded pistols and waded through the lounge strewn with broken plates and saucers.

'Police! Anyone here? We are responding to an emergency call.'

'In here.'

'Are you hurt?'

'No.'

Rose removed the bed that barricaded the bedroom door. Then she opened the door. She was relieved to see the two-armed police officers.

She narrated how Pastor Nehemiah had showed up at her flat wielding a gun and she had barricaded her bedroom. He had threatened to shoot her.

One of the officers advised Rose to go and hide somewhere safe until Pastor Nehemiah was apprehended. The other officer received an immediate call that Pastor Nehemiah had been sighted at his church. The two officers responded to the call.

Rose was left terrified. She went to hide at the flat of a neighbour. She phoned mum to tell her that she was safe.

Pastor Nehemiah's arrest was headline news on radio and tv stations. Rose was relieved that he was now in police custody. She returned to her flat and hired a handyman to fix the flat door.

That night Rose felt deep anger and resentment towards Pastor Nehemiah. She pondered what to do with the pregnancy. She rummaged through her handbag and found the piece of paper that Amy had scribbled an address; 27 Muzhanje road, Mufakose.

The old woman, Gogo Mavhu, who lived at the address, was well known in the high-density suburb for assisting women terminate pregnancies. But she wouldn't help Rose unless she correctly answered the question; 'What can I do for you, my daughter?' Amy had coached Rose on the correct response to the question. "You must respond, 'I am a chicken about to destroy my eggs.'

8

Rose took a day off work. She boarded a commuter omnibus from Harare city centre to Mufakose. She knew the high-density suburb well having grown up there.

She got off the commuter omnibus and looked for the house in the dusty streets of the suburb. She found the house and entered the gate. But Gogo Mavhu was not home. Her granddaughter went to fetch her from the vegetable market.

When Gogo arrived, she glared at Rose from scalp to shoe. 'What can I do for you, my daughter?'

'I am a chicken about to destroy my eggs.'

Gogo relaxed and smiled. She explained that backstreet abortions were illegal in the country, but she was only providing a service to women who needed it. 'Have you really taken time to think about your decision to have an abortion?'

'Yes.'

Gogo Mavhu led Rose into the kitchen. There she poured water into an empty plastic bottle of *Mazoe* crush. She put powdered herbs into the bottle and screwed on the cap. She shook the bottle until there was a frothy concoction in the bottle. She looked at Rose. 'If you drink this, it will immediately induce termination of your pregnancy.' She handed the bottle to Rose.

Rose gazed at the frothy concoction and hesitated. Her hands were trembling. She slowly raised the bottle to her mouth. She was about to drink when her phone rang. She stopped and put the bottle on the floor. She excused herself and rushed out of the kitchen.

'Are you all right, Rose. I had this nightmare last night, and saw you drowning, and I couldn't save you.'

'I am fine, mum. I am in the middle of doing something important,' Rose was stunned by the coincidence.

'Please call me when you are free. The nightmare troubled me.'

Rose returned to the kitchen. She gazed at Gogo Mavhu and the bottle of concoction. She extracted a five US dollar note and handed it to her. 'I am so sorry I can't go through with this,' she said. 'I have changed my mind.' Rose dashed out of the house.

Rose was bamboozled. *Why did mum phone her at the exact moment that she was about to take the concoction? Was this a sign, a warning of a bad omen, that she was putting her life and the baby in danger?*

***

That afternoon, Rose was relaxing in the lounge with mum when she received an anonymous call. She ignored it. There was a second call. She went outside and answered the call. 'Hello, Rose.'

'It's Mai Gumbo. I wanted to talk to you woman-to-woman.'

'About what?'

'Pastor Nehemiah asked me to phone you and express his sincere remorse for threatening you with a gun. He says he was in a bad place when he did that. He is sincerely sorry and asks for your forgiveness.'

'Forgiveness?'

'Yes, forgiveness.'

'I am not God who forgives transgressions.'

'That is all I wanted to say. Good day.' Mai Gumbo ended the call abruptly.

Rose returned to the lounge.

'Who called you?' mum asked.

'Someone called the wrong number.'

Rose was quiet. She wondered whether the call was a ploy to stop her from pressing further charges against Pastor Nehemiah.

Rose was done with men for the meantime. All she wanted was to endure the pain of a pregnancy that she almost terminated earlier in the day. She would give birth to the child and raise it on her own. Something good had come out of the affair with Pastor Nehemiah. She was relieved that she didn't terminate the pregnancy. She smiled lovingly at mum.

Acknowledgements

Thank you to Mr. Memory Chirere for reading my manuscript and for the constructive suggestions to improve my stories at the developmental edit stage. Thank you so much. *Ndatenda zvikuru, Mukuru, Musharukwa, VaChirere,* and congratulations on winning the National Arts Merit Award (NAMA) 2024 for Outstanding Poetry Book with *Shamhu yeZera Renyu.* Thanks to Samantha Rumbidzai Vazhure, NAMA winner 2023, for Outstanding Poetry Book with *Starfish Blossoms,* for your meticulous attention to detail at copy editing and proofreading, and Carnelian Heart Publishing for believing in my work; for publishing and promoting it. Thank you to my tutor, Mandy Pannett and Susie Busby, the Principal of The Writer's Bureau, for the support during the Novel and Short Story Writing Course. Thank you to the editor of Kalahari Review for publishing an earlier version of the short story, *Free at Last.* This short story has now been titled, *Out of the Lion's Den.* Thank you also to the editor Tendai Rinos Mwanaka for including an earlier version of my short story, *Tomb of the Unknown Soldier,* in Zimbolicious 8: anthology of Zimbabwean Literature and Arts (2023). I am very thankful to Sahwira, Andrew Chatora for your support with editing this short story collection, and also giving me the opportunity to edit your short story collection, *Inside Harare Alcatraz and Other short stories.* Iron sharpens iron. Thanks to the National Arts Council of Zimbabwe for unlocking the doors of my writing career with the NAMA for Outstanding First Creative Published Work (2023) for my first book, *The Mad Man on First Street and Other Short Stories.* I will always cherish the award. Thanks to my close family who take a close interest in my writing, Loveness, David (jnr) Tendai and Ropafadzo, Silver, Merylene and others. This is a gift for Anesu, *'Shushu, Nesu Nesu'*, my granddaughter. Thanks to close friends like Albert Mativenga, James Muramani and Stan Mukwenya. Above all, thanks to all the book readers around the world who have bought my first book and read it and viewed my YouTube videos explaining why I write. This second book is for you readers. I sincerely hope you will enjoy being lost in these stories. Finally, thanks to Jehovah who bestowed on me the passion for writing.

Biography of David Chasumba

David Chasumba is an award-winning Zimbabwean Author and Poet. His debut short story collection, *The Mad Man on First Street and Other Short Stories*, won the NAMA (National Arts Merit Award) in 2023 for Outstanding First Creative Published Work in Zimbabwe. His short stories have been published in Kalahari Review and in five anthologies; Zimbolicious 8, an anthology of Zimbabwean Literature and Arts; A Bundle of Joy and Other Short Stories from Africa; Momaya Short Story Review: (Treasure) (2015); Small Worlds anthology- University of Brighton Literature Society (2014) and Reflections anthology- University of Brighton Literature Society (2015). His short story, Crossing the

Rubicon, was longlisted for the Fish Publishing Short Story Competition (2013-14). David has published poems in Kalahari Review, in British Haiku Society anthology (2023), and in Ipikai Poetry Journal, including Issue 5 in memory of Dambudzo Marechera. David holds two MA degrees in Media and Cultural Studies and Social Work from University of Sussex and Canterbury Christ Church University respectively. David is passionate about diversity in writing and publishing, and he is a member of Writing Our Legacy. David lives in Bexhill on sea, East Sussex England. X: @davidchasumba22